SPOOKED

31 DAYS OF TRICK OR TREAT - BIKERS & MOBSTERS

MANDA MELLETT

SPOOKED

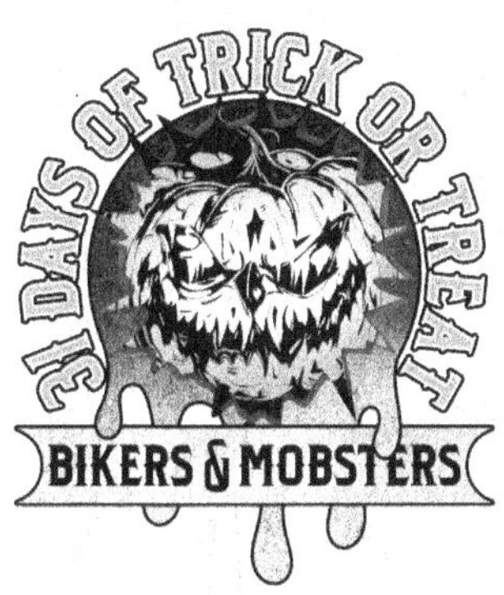

COPYRIGHT

Disclaimer

This book is firmly set in the fictional world. Names, characters, businesses, places, events and incidents are either the products of the author's imagination or used in a fictitious manner. Any resemblance to actual persons, living or dead, or actual events is purely coincidental.

Warning

This book is dark in places and contains content of a sexual, abusive and violent nature. It may not be suitable for persons under the age of 18.

NO AI was used to produce this book. The words and story come straight from the author's mind. The cover image is of a real model and designed by human hands.

CONTRIBUTORS

Photographer Golden Czermak

Model Hunter Harden

Cover Design by CT Cover Creations

Edited and formatted by Maggie Kern @ Ms.K Edits

Proof reading by Darlene Tallman

BLURB

Blurb

After a bad motorcycle crash put the leading riders, the current officers of the Satan's Devils MC out of action, the FOG, or the previous officers recently retired, step up to temporarily run the club again.

Unable to ride or perform his sergeant-at-arms duties, once Hound is released from the hospital, he's bored, and looking for something to occupy himself. He offers his assistance at any of the Satan's Devil's business that might need help. SD Construction has a job that's ideal for a one-legged man with a TBI.

Said work sends him to a decaying, long abandoned mansion, with the instructions to take photos which show whether it's restorable or should be demolished. Hound quickly finds reasons why the project's been turned down by most other construction companies in the area.

After vowing he'd never return, while reporting back to Shooter and Bullet, a pretty woman enters the office. She claims she was brought up in that house, and insists she be given a tour around it. Hound tries to satisfy her with photos, but one picture captures something he hadn't seen with his naked eye.

Despite his reluctance to return to the mansion, he finds it hard to resist Maeve's appeal to have one last chance to visit her old home.

Perhaps he should have stayed away, as the Satan's Devils find themselves embroiled against an enemy, the likes of which they've never encountered before.

And, is Maeve exactly what she seems?

Amazon.com: My Book
Amazon.co.uk: My Book
Amazon.ca: My Book
Amazon.com.au: My Book

PROLOGUE
HOUND

It should have been a nice ride out, no backpacks, and none of the old ladies who have their own bikes either. Just us brothers, enjoying the wind in our faces. The day is clear, not a cloud in the sky, making me feel like hollering into the air simply because it's such a great moment to be alive. This is the life that I live for. The freedom of the road, the rush of the pavement beneath my wheels and the thundering of the engine between my legs.

As sergeant-at-arms, I'm riding just behind my prez, Wizard, and alongside Hawk, the VP. Behind us come the rest of the officers, then members without official club standing. After them, at the end of our pack, where they wanted to be, the F.O.G.s, Fucking Old Guys, the previous highest-ranking officers of the club, the men who'd stepped back a couple of years ago to let the younger guys take over. After years of steering the helm, Drummer, our ex-prez, who'd rebuilt the club almost from scratch when his dad, Bastard, had lost his life in a raid by the Feds, had decided he wanted to spend his golden years without the responsibility of the gavel. His resignation was swiftly followed by Peg, my predecessor as sergeant-at-arms, and Wraith, the VP. While they had left in the prime of their lives, Blade had no choice but to stand down. The arthritis in his hands sadly meant he was unable to continue in the role of enforcer. I've often wondered whether the others had taken the demotion to soften the blow to Blade.

I'd prospected under them, served under them respectfully for several years, and admit to feeling overwhelmed when they stepped back. I somehow became the sergeant-at-arms—a position I'd thought I'd have waited a lifetime to become vacant. Wizard, Hawk, Throttle and I had quickly formed a tight team.

Our predecessors? Well, fuck. The F.O.G.s had become pains in our asses and even resembled unruly kids at times. Unshackled from their previous responsibilities, their new purpose in life seemed to leave them with only one goal—to seek enjoyment. Sometimes that meant them kicking back against the new regime and behaving more like unruly prospects. I suspected it was all a ruse to test their new leaders. It's hard not to wonder whether the men who'd bought the t-shirts and had already been there and done that were checking to see if we were up to scratch. I don't know about the other recently appointed officers, but I sometimes feel I'm walking on eggshells, having to prove myself.

The autumn sun beats down, a bearable temperature compared to summer. My hands, feet and attention coordinate on autopilot, the synchronised dance of riding alongside my brothers in formation now second nature. As the thunder of the engines blocks out all other sounds, the steady throb of the pavement beneath my wheels enables my mind to wander.

There's a curve to my lips as I think back. It's been twenty-plus years since I first joined the club as a snotty-nosed young prospect, and the following twelve months had made me a man. The Satan's Devils were good to me, well, maybe they acted a bit shit at times before I patched in, but it was some of the experiences of the older members—the F.O.G.s that I'm currently riding in front of—that had me wanting to spread my wings. With their encouragement and blessing, I'd joined the Marines, did my eight years, saw things no human being should be subjected to, breathed the smell of fear and death, and experienced losses that many men wouldn't be able to recover from. I'd been luckier than most, knowing I had a safety net to fall into.

When I returned home, I was beyond grateful that I had this ready-made family to anchor me, who accepted all my mental and physical war wounds and welcomed me back with open arms. Unlike many of my brothers I'd served with, who never saw their home soil again, or came back to nothing and no one to support them.

Handed the cut that I'd already earned, I was embraced into the ranks of these brothers. I'd been nineteen when I was first patched. Twenty-seven when I ended my service. Thirty-nine when I became Peg's replacement.

I'd been content as a member, shocked as fuck when all the officers had decided it was time to resign, and completely blown away when I'd been nominated. It had meant more than any commendations I'd earned in service.

Humbled by the honour they'd bestowed on me, every day since, I've strived to be the best I could be, never forgetting how much responsibility had landed on my and my newly made-up brothers' shoulders. As time passed, I could also appreciate the lightness our predecessors felt having passed on the mantle to the younger generation.

Two years after being promoted, I feel I've settled into my role, believe I deserve it and spend less time questioning my abilities and whether I'm the right person for the job.

The wind whistling past my face is warming, not cooling, and the monsoon season's behind us. Autumn is showing signs of taking a grip on the land as the leaves fall like snow and the colours change all around. Keeping a steady pace behind Wizard, I cast a glance toward Hawk and give him a grin and a wave of my hand. His answering nod confirms that he, too, is simply enjoying the freedom of the day.

This is exactly what being a biker should be. Freedom and the pure pleasure of being on the road.

Fuck! Shit! Wizard's bike starts swerving, and suddenly he goes down, metal screaming in protest as his bike slides horizontally. Instinctively, I press down on the foot brake while simultaneously gripping hard on the front. I also lose control, trying to evade Wizard's downed bike as Hawk crashes into mine. I've a split second to notice the tanker on its side a hundred yards in front of me, and to breathe in the fumes of the diesel that covers the road before I'm skidding sideways along the road, my bike on top of me...

CHAPTER ONE
HOUND

"Bullshit!" My eyes spit fire at Drummer and Peg, men I've looked up to most of my adult life but who are currently seriously annoying me.

Uh uh. There's the glare I've often seen my former prez give to people he's about to kill, and I'm unable to deny that it doesn't have a chilling effect as it's directed at me. I can't exactly piss myself as I currently have a catheter coming out of my dick, but I'd take a guess that the container beneath the bed has a suddenly increased volume of yellow liquid. I watch, swallowing fast, as Peg puts his hand on Drummer's shoulder, then, when he gets his attention, gives him a shake of his head.

When the ex-prez addresses me next, it's almost worse—it's condescending, as though he's explaining things to a six-year-old. "Hound, you had a head injury that scrambled your brains and put you in a coma for three weeks. You were touch-and-go for a while, and you've only just come back to us. You've got more than enough metal in your leg to set off any detectors around. You can't even walk, let alone ride your fuckin' bike. You need time to heal. It's only temporary, but Peg *is* going to be stepping up in your place, acting as sergeant-at-arms."

"Who the fuck do you think you are?" I growl. "You're not my prez. You can't order me around."

Drummer's quiet manner disappears as fast as it had come, and his face grows red. Peg steps forward, glaring at the ex-prez, and continues in a conciliatory tone, "Wizard's in an even worse place than you are. Well..." he stops and snorts. "Same place, a few doors down, but both of his legs are in traction."

Taking a deep breath, I realise with a fuckton of guilt, that only newly conscious, my first thought hadn't been to wonder whether my brothers had been injured. But then, it's only been minutes since I opened my eyes, and less than that to discover I'd been unconscious for three weeks. Interpreting what Drummer had said, it seems I'd suffered from a traumatic brain injury.

After exhaling a long sigh, Drummer takes over the narrative again. His tone, influenced by Peg's, is decidedly softer. "Wizard and I spoke when he came out of surgery." He pauses, his eyes focusing on mine, making sure I'm listening. I dip my head to confirm that I am. "He asked me to step back up and lead the club as he's going to be out of action for some time." He gives a mirthless huff. "Maybe it wouldn't have been so bad had it just been him, but Hawk's broken a fair few ribs, and also needs time to heal. At *Wizard's* request," he puts emphasis on those words, with a raise of his eyebrow, checking I understand, "Wraith has retaken the VP spot for now."

I swallow as saliva fills my mouth. *Fuck, this is serious.* My recollection of the accident is hazy, almost nonexistent. I'd first thought, *hoped* maybe, I was the only one to go down. "Throttle?" I rasp.

"Broke his fuckin' collarbone. Did it good and proper too. He's in a brace and they're talking physical therapy." Due to his prior comments, his next revelation comes as no surprise. "Blade's taking over now, or at least in a guiding role if not hands-on."

I jerk as the realisation of how selfish I've been comes into my head, and I stammer my next question out hesitantly. "A-anyone else injured, or…"

"No one died," Peg reassures me fast. His voice softens. "Mouse wrenched his shoulder trying to stop his bike from going down. But apart from everyone else needing a good shot of whisky to combat the shock, no others were harmed." He gives me a beat to let that sink in. "You remember what happened?"

Closing my eyes, I think back, bringing it to the forefront of my mind, sifting through images that flood through my head, a kaleidoscope of indistinct memories. "We were out on a ride…" I fight to recall, but other than my remembered pleasure of the day and the perfect riding conditions, there's nothing else that comes to mind. Defeated, I shake my head, then regret the action as a blast of pain shoots through me. "Who the fuck attacked us?" It shows just how scrambled my brain actually is that it's only now I ask the most pertinent question of them all. One which should have occurred first to a sergeant-at-arms.

"No one." At Peg's words, my eyes open wide. With a grimace, he expands, "Wrong fuckin' place, wrong fuckin' time. Tanker driver had a micro-sleep at the wheel, overcorrected, and the tanker went down on its side, sliding up the road. Just out of view, up around the bend. Diesel all over the road."

"Diesel?"

Drummer's head bob confirms Peg's words.

My sergeant-at-arms' mind races. "Could have been made to look like an accident. Someone could have been targeting us."

Placing his hand lightly on my shoulder, Drummer tells me more. "It was a huge mess—injured bodies, bits of bike everywhere, tanker blocking the road. Had to get the cops involved." The twist of his mouth shows how much he didn't like that. "Seems it was just an accident, down to the driver's inattention." His eyes fix on mine. "I know you want someone to fight for this, but we've looked into it, and there's nothing beneath the surface. Mouse hacked into the company's records and found evidence that the driver took his eyes off the road. He also found he'd been driving too many hours, but on the route exactly as planned. We'd told no one our plans. No one knew we'd be riding that road at that time."

Peg's raising and dipping his head in confirmation. "Brother, it was like some macabre version of Skittles. Wizard lost control of his bike, and Hawk and you did the same slip and slide. Throttle fought hard, but he too went down. Mouse, Heart, and Dollar managed to slow, but crashed into your wrecks, though they were mainly unharmed." He lets out a shuddering sigh. "Took a few fuckin' years off my life."

"Yours?" Drummer raises a brow. He swallows tightly. "Seeing brothers," he glances at Peg, "our kids, go down? Fuckin' never want to experience that again. Hound, you better believe if we had anyone to blame other than an asshole taking his eyes off the road, then we'd still be torturing them in the storeroom now."

Momentarily, I wonder what was worse—being knocked out and unaware of what was happening or being forced to watch the disaster as it occurred.

That doesn't make me feel any better. "What about the driver?" I still want someone to blame.

Drummer rakes his fingers back through his hair. "Man, he was a fuckin' mess. Puking up all over the road."

"You let him walk away?" I'm incredulous.

"Cops were there," Drummer explains. As I open my mouth, he shakes his head. "They arrested him."

I think he should have gotten a fucking beatdown at least. My scowl must convey my thoughts.

"Hey, we were too busy picking up broken bodies and bikes to pay him any attention. And who do you think fingers would be pointed at if, after he was released, we'd taken him out? Brother, got more things to worry about than revenge on an over-tired trucker who doesn't even live in the same state."

"And," Drummer adds, "he's very much unemployed now."

I suppose that's something.

My brain seems overly slow to tick into action, not knowing the pertinent questions to ask. I realise I don't have any idea how long it will be before I can get back on my bike, which brings me to another concern. "What happened to my ride?"

Drummer seems more comfortable now that he's on more solid ground. "Back at the compound. Blade's doing what he can to fix yours and the other bikes. Heart and Mouse are talking to the tanker company about compensation. It looks like they're going to pay up, but it's going to take time."

Godfuckingdamnit! I'm without a bike and without a working leg. At this point, there's surely a question mark about how much my brain's been fucked up. I realise now, despite my earlier horror about the F.O.G.s moving back into their previous roles, my brothers know what they're doing. While it really hurts to give up the role I'd been so proud to achieve, realizing I won't be capable of giving it my all until I heal, I surrender. "I'll step back." My eyes meet Peg's.

I can tell it hadn't been in question. Drummer's back in the hot seat now, and it will be his decision. But Peg's chin lift tells me he's accepting my capitulation, both of us pretending that I really had any say.

"I'm still a member, though?" I'd earned my fucking patch. I wouldn't give it up without argument.

Drummer rears back as if I'd thrown a punch at him. Which, of course, at the moment I can't. I've got tubes and lines coming out of me everywhere, anchoring me to the hospital equipment that had presumably kept me alive.

"Of course you're still a fuckin' member, same way the others are. All we're doing is stepping up to take care of club business to give you a chance to heal." Drummer's staring at me as if I insulted him. He adds gruffly, "Got your cut waiting for you whenever you're ready for it."

"I'm just keeping your seat warm, Brother," Peg assures me as seriously as if he's taking a vow. "Until you're fit enough to take it up again."

When he reaches out his hand, I only hesitate for a moment before clasping it in mine, telling him honestly, "Know you will, Brother."

"Gentlemen, visiting time is over," a nurse says as she enters the room. I'd like to say she's gorgeous, and someone I'm going to have wet dreams about. But, hey, lucky me, my nurse has about twenty years on me, making her near retirement age. If I hadn't previously understood how women could be described as battle-axes before, I certainly do now.

Even Drummer almost salutes as he responds sharply, "Yes, ma'am."

Then he and Peg disappear out of the door, leaving me to her mercy.

In truth, I don't give a damn how the nurse looks or how old she is, as long as she's proficient at her job and gets me out of here as quickly as possible. I hate being cooped up, especially in a hospital. Moreover, I don't like the thought that I've lost all dignity by my bladder emptying directly into a tube without even feeling the urge to piss. *What if, when they remove the catheter, I'll find I no longer have control?* I shudder as that possibility occurs to me. I'd never given a thought that Depends might be in my near future. Now that that thought's planted in my brain, it's all I can think about. I force myself to consider the plus points. I'd be able to ride my Harley all day without stopping other than to refuel the tank. *Uh uh.* No way. What woman would want to give it up to a man wearing diapers?

Fuck my life.

As Nurse Voldemort completes her assessment of my vitals, I swallow down asking about my future ability to pee, as another, more urgent, question bursts out of me. "When am I going to be allowed out of here?"

Instead of answering directly, she consults the tablet she's holding in her hand. "Mr. Ockenden." I cringe at my government name. "Now that you're conscious and your readings are in a good range, I suspect you'll be released as soon as our PT therapists assess you can use crutches." She chuckles, but it sounds evil, not full of mirth. "I do see a lot of physical therapy in your future."

Maybe, but it won't be by visiting the hospital. No way. As soon as I'm back at the club, I'll rely on our own resources. Back in the day, Peg got Sophie, Wraith, our old VP's, *present one now, I remind myself,* woman, out of a wheelchair and walking again on a prosthetic after she lost her leg. I'd trust him more than any of these hospital quacks any day, even though he'll be one hell of a taskmaster.

In many ways, I'm glad I spent the last three weeks unconscious. Hell, I'd never heal if I'd been aware of how many times the nurses come in to disturb my sleep. Then, when I finally fall deep enough to find myself some REM, the breakfast tray comes rattling around at an ungodly hour, waking me yet again. Inwardly, I scream, *just get me out of here.*

I think I could have gone crazy had not a man and a woman walked in wearing different colour scrubs. Apparently, they are my physiotherapists. After waiting for the nurse to get that demeaning catheter removed, I'm given a lesson on crutches and an exam concerning stairs, which I'm determined to pass. After I've successfully mastered putting my weight on one leg and using the aids to swing my metal-enhanced leg forward, they sign off on some paperwork. And, bonus, I didn't wet myself.

Whatever magic they've conjured, it results in a doctor appearing, giving me the semi-good news that they want to keep me a little longer to monitor the immediate effects my traumatic brain injury might have caused. Like a good boy, I nodded, raised my chin, shook my head side to side, or whatever their explanation warranted. Most of their conversation went right over my head when they talked about possible headaches, fatigue, memory loss, lack of ability to concentrate, or balance problems. Apparently, it was on the cards that I could suffer confusion, difficulties with puzzle solving, or a hundred different things.

Yeah, yeah. I feel fine. Sure, my head hurts, but that's only the aftereffects of where I cracked my skull on the ground. It's a case of picking myself up, brushing myself down, and getting myself reestablished as sergeant-at-arms as soon as I can. I'm a man. I can survive a little knock. All the warnings go in one ear and straight out the other.

I behave. I do everything asked of me, frustrated that their fucking monitors don't lie. It's only when they're finally satisfied that my stats have stabilised that they tell me I can go home the next day, subject to any overnight deteriorations in my condition. You better believe that I willed my blood pressure to stay low, and my heartbeat to remain normal.

Having successfully achieved that task, I place a call that

summons Razza, one of our prospects. As soon as he appears, I hurry him along to execute my escape before the medics can come up with an excuse to make me stay.

Before I leave, I get him to wheel me along to the room where Wizard is being kept prisoner. Even though I've been told of his injuries, I hiss as I see him lying with both legs held in the air, and Amy, his old lady, fussing around him. The sight hits me like a kick to the teeth. Here I'm complaining about going home on crutches, and he's got no imminent release date. More accepting than I am of the situation, his comment that he'd rather be this way than dead does knock some sense into me. Even more so when he goes on to explain why he's surprisingly sanguine about Drummer and the other fucking old guys taking over the officer roles in the club, pointing out to me that we all need to heal before we can resume our duties. The fact that he's so adamant it's only a matter of time has me feeling easier in my mind, relieved it's not me letting the side down.

After promises to visit again soon, I get Razza to take me home.

CHAPTER TWO
HOUND

Home. The Satan's Devils' compound. Many years back, a wildfire had all but destroyed a vacation resort just outside of Tucson. Spurned by most people, the Satan's Devils had purchased the property cheap, spending their time, blood, sweat and tears to do it up so it's the envy of all chapters of our club. Suites for each member, a swimming pool—it originally had three, but one was filled in and the third, was covered over and is now our weapons store, undiscovered despite numerous Fed searches of the club. At the top end of the compound, we've extra land extending into the foothills of the Coronado Mountains, where many members, including myself, have built our homes. It's an ideal location to recover, a bolthole of my own, and a nearby clubhouse where help can always be found.

A strong family vibe hangs over the club. Since first adopting this as their home, the Satan's Devils have gained old ladies aplenty and numerous kids as a result. Some of the F.O.G.s even have grandchildren. Of course, we still have sweetbutts for the single men, but as we're few in number now, they have to do other duties outside of performing on their backs.

I sigh with relief as the prospect drives me through the gates, and don't protest as he continues up to the clubhouse on the track, which is normally reserved only for two-wheel transport. After helping me out of the truck and ensuring I'm balanced on my crutches, he swiftly makes a three-point turn and disappears to park alongside the other cages behind our auto shop.

"Hey, Brother! Told you to keep the shiny side up." Sporting a shit-eating grin, Rock comes over and pulls me into him, unbalancing me as he slaps my back.

"Careful, fucker." Marvel comes close and, with a hand to my forearm, sets me straight. "Good to see you back on your fee... foot." His lips curve in a similar way to our brother's.

Next, it's Joker, with his arm around Lady's shoulder, stepping up. "You look like death, Brother." Well, if I expected anything positive, I'm to be disappointed.

But hope looms for a second as Lady elbows his man. "Nah, he looks the picture of health." Then, turning to Joker, he adds, soto voce, "Dead man walking."

"Fuckers," I snarl.

"Hey, easy on him, Brothers. Man who cheated the grave can't help how he looks." Dollar steps forward and, with his hand on my back, gently encourages me in the direction I want to go—toward the bar.

I'm stopped on the way by the faint whirring of a mobility scooter. As I stand back to let our longest serving prospect pass, I note Tommy's looking healthier than when I'd last seen him. He's got more colour and his lingering chest infection that had us so worried seems to have, at last, passed.

He stops in front of me and beckons to my leg. "Hound's got an owie."

"Sure have, Brother," I respond. "But it will mend."

Tommy chuckles and points to his scooter. "You could get one of these." He's so damn proud of his ride that's made to resemble a Harley. I can't snarl or tell him I'd rather be dead first. Instead, I offer a grin and a nod, tilt my head toward the bar, and, taking the hint, the whirr starts again as Tommy moves out of my way.

At last, I'm in touching distance of what I've been longing for. Alcohol might not be the best thing, but that's what I demand, not giving a damn that it might not mix well with my meds. As I awkwardly get my ass on a bar stool, I nod to the man who comes up by my side.

"How you doing, Hawk?"

In response, he winces, wrapping his arms around his chest. "Broken ribs suck," he informs me. I grimace in sympathy.

"Hi, Hound." Olivia, Hawk's old lady, steps in close, eyeing me carefully, then plants a kiss on my cheek, an action that elicits a growl from her man. "It's good to have you home." She then whispers something in Hawk's ear, which has him grinning. Offering me a salute as a goodbye, the pair turns to leave the clubhouse. Doesn't take a genius to figure out she's just offered him something he can't refuse.

Fuck, I don't even think I could cope with a blow job right now. Probably make my skull explode.

As Jekyll takes his place, I pre-empt any comment on my appearance, but, having noticed who's not around, ask, "How's Throttle doing?"

Jekyll smirks. "He was here earlier, then Gwen pulled him away to nurse him back to health." From his nudge and wink, I have to assume at least Throttle's dick is in working order.

One by one, other brothers and their old ladies step up, either to give me shit or offer sympathy relative to their gender. I tap the bar. Butcher, the prospect on duty tonight, places what must be my fourth shot of Jack in front of me without me having to ask.

Whether it's the alcohol or me being upright for so long in weeks, I soon feel myself fading.

"Whoa, Bro." Bullet notices I'm about to fall off the stool. "Let's get you situated so you can get some rest."

I don't want to be treated like an invalid, but I have to accept that's what I am. Despondently, I accept Bullet's assistance to get my crutches under me, and stagger a little as I try to take my own weight. *Maybe the Jack wasn't such a good idea after all.* Knowing I won't be able to navigate the distance up to my house without help, I don't complain as Bullet continues to offer aid. The short distance feels like a marathon, and having reached my limits, as my only thought is getting to my bed and crashing, I don't object when he helps me up the stairs and into my bedroom. Thankfully, he leaves me alone to undress.

Once he's gone, I collapse onto my bed, utterly worn out from the day's exertions. It's not long before I realise the benefit of the catheter I'd so despised, now it's gone. My bladder is full, but to go to the en suite bathroom, I've got to get my crutches under me once again. *Fuck my life.* I hate this. Hate being disabled. Hate that I can't be the sergeant-at-arms, can't prove that I can look out for the club when I can barely look after myself. And that sleep I looked forward to, uninter-rupted by visits of nurses? Nowhere to be found. I tossed and turned all night.

The next day dawns, and if anything, my mood becomes worse. I attend the weekly church, having to watch Peg back in the seat that I'd earned, worrying that the old man might get too comfortable there and decide to permanently come out of retirement and stay. It's not as if the meeting is interesting, being basic business. Our now four-week-old accident was put down as just that, and seemingly forgotten. I'd rather have an enemy I could face and blame for making me as useless as I am. But it appears there's nothing I can rail against. When I try to come up with a reason they should continue their investigation, every suggestion I make, every lead I suggest, has already been exhausted and dismissed.

Not one for being idle, the next day I take myself laboriously down to the shop where I usually work, but Blade soon shoos me away. Although both of my arms are in working order, my reliance on crutches means I'm a liability rather than a help. My gut clenches at the sight of my bike in pieces, knowing she can be put back together, but hating to see others doing the rebuild that I'm currently unable to do. I hop/limp away and run into Peg in the clubhouse. When I ask him to help me with my physical therapy, he informs me he's spoken to my doctors, and they've advised I'm not to put too much strain on my leg until the bones have fused.

Fuck my life.

I return to my house and watch mindless television, finding nothing that holds my interest for more than a short while. When I attempt to find company, even being at the clubhouse annoys me, brothers going about their business without the handicaps that I suffer. Throttle makes an appearance, along with Hawk. Both of them seem happy their old ladies are coddling them and not looking like they're missing their commitments one bit. When I find myself envying Tommy's ease of movement using his mobility scooter to get around, I give up on seeking out company, return to my house, and go to bed early. I feel like a failure, unable to will my body to heal faster than even I know is physically possible.

Sunday passes in much the same vein. When the sun rises on yet another day, I wake, feeling so out of sorts, I realise I can't go on like this. I'm not used to inactivity, to feeling useless, having nothing to do, and having no purpose. As I assess my options, it occurs to me that while I can't ride a bike, it's my left leg that's immobile, and although I hate the feeling of being trapped in a cage, I can still drive.

The hospital had seemed like a prison to me, and the compound feels constricting as well. I can't work in the shop, but perhaps I can contribute in one of our other businesses in Tucson? A waiter on crutches would be worth fuck, so the Wheel Inn, our bar and restaurant, is out. There's never a lack of brothers willing to help out at the Satan's Angels strip club, and as a bouncer, I'd be shit right now, so I don't even contemplate that. At our tattoo shop? Fuck no. I'd send business away rather than gain it, which leaves SD Construction. I'm desperate, surely there's something I could do there. Maybe showing prospective customers around some of the malls we've built, or other successful businesses? Hell, even answering phones on reception would be better than the nothing I'm doing now.

It's more the thought of gaining some independence, rather than optimism that I'd actually be a help to anyone, that gets me into one of the club's SUVs and heading into Tucson. Glancing up at the building as I approach, I can't help but feel admiration. The offices of SD Construction are impressive, even to my untrained eyes. It's one of the club's oldest and main achievements, with a solid reputation and is gaining in respectability since Zane, Drummer's second son, joined them as a quickly rising, respected architect.

I feel out of place as I push open the glass door and enter the air-conditioned reception. When I approach the desk and give my name, it feels like only seconds before Shooter appears, clasping my hand, pulling me in for a back slap and leading me to the elevator. He presses the button, which takes us to the floor where it's immediately apparent the main business is done. I follow him into an impressive office, the walls draped with design drawings and photos. Bullet stands, comes toward me, and greets me in the same way Shooter had just done. He pulls back, and as he assesses me, I realise the last time he'd seen me was when he'd put me to bed on Thursday night. His quick nod lets me know he sees an improvement in my condition. Without uttering the tedious enquiries about my health, for which I'm eternally grateful, he motions me to a comfortable-looking chair, and assists me by taking my crutches and propping them against the wall.

It's Shooter who speaks first. "Good to see you back on your feet." He pauses, quickly changing his chuckle into a more polite cough before he corrects, "Foot. To what do we owe this dubious pleasure?"

"Asshole," I huff into my hand, but make sure it's loud enough for him to hear me.

Shooter shrugs. "Can't recall you ever visiting before."

Bullet barks a laugh. "No need to ask why, Brother. Before, he wasn't cursed with limited mobility and could do anything he wanted. Riding, fixing bikes and breaking heads is more our sergeant-at-arms' style." His shrewd eyes narrow. "I'm betting you're bored," he surmises correctly. Then he grins. "Just so happens we have a job that we could use some input on."

Shooter's brows shoot up to his hairline. "We have?"

Ignoring him and focusing on his business partner, I make my voice casual. "Yeah?" I try for a disinterested tone, rather than appear to be the overly eager broken man attempting to be useful again.

Bullet's attention turns to Shooter, who's still looking perplexed. He utters just two words, which have the effect of Shooter's face brightening like the sun suddenly reappearing from behind clouds. "Sullivan House."

Shooter wastes no time leaping to his feet, approaching a

filing cabinet, and rifling through it before finally selecting one and tossing the file at me while grinning widely.

Automatically catching the cardboard folder, I make sure no papers fall out. For a moment, I just stare at the documents in my hand. I wanted something to do, but the fact they've come up with this so fast makes me suspicious, and Shooter's gleeful reaction has me wondering just what the hell type of job they could have for a disabled man.

CHAPTER THREE
HOUND

Tentatively opening the file as warily as if I were approaching a nervous dog, I slide out the papers. I spare a glance at Shooter, then Bullet, both men who've been far longer in the club than I have, and in the construction business for twenty years or more. Both men's expressions are now blank and guarded, and neither gives me comfort this isn't some kind of hazing. It makes me doubt why I bothered to come here. If I'm useless as a mechanic, what the fuck did I think I could offer to the club's construction business, of which I know nothing except for the dollars it adds to our bottom line?

While not retired officers, Bullet and Shooter have been Devils since well before my time. They're F.O.G.s in everything but name and, like the others, fucking with younger brothers is often their game. *They wouldn't do that to an injured comrade, would they?*

I don't fucking know. But mentally preparing myself for the worst while having absolutely no idea what might have landed in my hands, I steel myself to look down, inwardly relieved when I note the first page is an innocent picture. It's just a house. I sigh with relief, then examine it some more. The word "house" barely describes it. It's a goddamn mansion—colonial style, with columns, not that common around here, more akin to the East Coast. Studying it closer, it appears to have been abandoned for years. Overgrown creepers cover the front and block light from some of the windows. As for the grounds, I suspect they were once expansive and manicured, but now nature's taken over, and what's left of any previous glamour has all disappeared.

I'm puzzled. What the fuck am I supposed to do with this? I won't get any more information unless I ask. Fixing my gaze on Bullet, I query, "What do you need doing?" *And how could I, who knows nothing about architecture or construction, possibly help?*

"Direct and to the point." Shooter grins at his partner, or one of them, I belatedly remind myself. Drummer's younger son, Zeke, has a full interest in the company, though he isn't present at the meeting. Strangely, in my view, he has never shown any inclination to become a patched Devil.

Shooter sits forward. "You want us to be straight with you?" His shrug is accompanied by a shake of his head. "Truth is, we don't rightly know. The owner of that mansion wants it razed to the ground, but we want to do an assessment. Could be it's worth renovating, in which case the club could buy it from her and do the work."

"I'm no structural engineer," I remind them. "Isn't this more in Zeke's field?" He's one for real. Got all the certificates to prove it.

"Zeke's snowed under with all the work coming in, and this is a bit of a mystery."

"Yeah," Bullet takes over. "Bitch has offered us a sum that's way over the top for a simple assessment. Raised red flags, you know?" Without waiting for me to give an acknowledgment, he picks it up again. "Got Mouse to look into it."

The decades the two men have been working together are obvious as Shooter seamlessly takes over. "We're her last resort. She's been through every construction firm in Tucson, and even as far away as Phoenix."

My eyes widen. "They all turned that job down?"

"No." Bullet retakes pole position. "They all took the job, went on site, and then turned tail and ran." He pre-empts my next question. "We've no fuckin' idea why." He raises his chin at Shooter.

I suppose it's a telltale sign of how long they've worked together, Shooter taking over as full partner after Viper died. They've got a kind of double act going on, making my head swing from one to the other as if watching a tennis match.

"We've felt them out but gotten no clear answer. The job's not worth what she's willing to pay." Bullet snorts and Shooter rolls his eyes at him. "It's either too much work for them to cope with, or too small and not worth their time."

"So, she upped the ante and came to us," I surmise. Fuck, I served as a Marine and a sergeant-at-arms now. Give me weapons to acquire, or people to protect and I'm your man. I know nothing about building, structural defects, or anything of that ilk. How would I be able to assess if the job is too big or too small? Admitting defeat, I shake my head. "Thanks, Brothers, for thinking I might be able to help you out, but I'm not sure that I can." I start to reach for my crutches, knowing they're busy and I need to get out of their hair.

Shooter holds up his hand. "Brother, you can do this. We're this deep," he holds his hand to his chin, "in work. Can't spare anyone to check this house out when, as everyone else has turned it down, it's likely to be a complete waste of time. To be blunt, we can't see any point in us sparing someone qualified to check it out. Was going to let it go before you came along." He chuckles. "Don't like refusing good money, and you've got time on your hands. All we're asking is that you go to the property and photograph everything that you can."

"Don't expect you to make an assessment, Bro, that's down to us," Bullet adds reassuringly.

Narrowing my eyes, I clarify, "Just go there and take pictures?"

Both men nod, giving satisfied grins like teachers whose pupil has answered a question correctly.

Rolling my head back on my shoulders, I sigh deeply. "Drummer's asked you to keep me occupied, hasn't he?"

They don't even bother to look sheepish. As one, they both answer in the affirmative, then turn to each other and grin. Shooter gestures to Bullet that he should speak next.

"Yeah. You're apparently getting under everyone's feet at the compound." He pauses to chuckle. "But, Brother, this ain't made-up work. It's really something we want to look at. At the end of the day, it probably isn't worth considering, as we've so many good-paying projects on the go. The fact that no one else wants the job raises suspicions from the start. We probably wouldn't even bother to check it out, but you're a gift horse we can't look in the mouth. You've got time, and if you've got the inclination, then I'm not kidding you, you'd be doing us a solid."

Staring at the photo one more time, I consider their situation. If they didn't have me at their disposal, they wouldn't even consider taking this job on? Maybe the place would have to be demolished, but it's one fine-looking mansion, a piece of history, something that should be treasured. *If* SD Construction could restore it to its prior glory, it would be one more feather in their cap, one more level of expertise they could lay claim to.

It might be just "made-up work", but maybe I could add something of value. I clarify again, "I just walk around and take pictures?" Before giving them a chance to answer, I again study the photo. Tapping my full leg cast, I warn them, "I might not be able to go everywhere if stairs are missing, or there are holes in the floors."

Bullet throws up his hands as if horrified. "Wouldn't fuckin' ask you to, Brother. Top priority is your healing and protecting yourself. You take pictures of anything you're able to access. That will be enough."

Shooter sighs. "Whatever you can do, Hound. I hate turning down work, but rather that than having you injure yourself."

"Any timescale?"

Together, they shake their heads. "As soon as you're ready, and take all the time you need. While the client's desperate for someone to take this job on, having exhausted all other options, they won't be rushing us if we say we need space to assess it all properly."

While I still have doubts I'm the right man, I'm desperate to do something, anything, that gets me out of the headspace I've been in since I'd laid my bike down. Having been demoted, while it might not be true, I feel I have to prove myself all over again. As a prospect, I was expected to do anything the club asked of me. Years down the line, that hasn't changed since I became a patched member, or lately, as an officer of the club. I'll never let my brothers down.

If I've been asked, I'll do it. Whatever doubts I might have are pushed to the back of my mind.

My decision isn't hard. "I'll go there tomorrow."

Shooter grins, pulls open a desk drawer and extracts something. When he hands it over to me, I see it's a bunch of keys. "Looking forward to seeing what you find out, Hound."

Something occurs to me. "You got a fancy camera I should use? An SLR or something?"

Bullet cackles. "You've got a fuckin' phone, Bro."

I do. But I also have to try to remember how to take photos. My job is, *was*, to protect the club. I usually don't have time, reason, or need to document my life through pictures. I suppose it's just point and snap, and hope for the best.

One thing's for certain. When I take on a job, I do it to the best of my ability and beyond. I'm determined to get SD Construction all that they need.

Bullet, Shooter and I shoot the shit for a while, then, knowing they're busy, I take my leave. As I exit the company office building, I'm certain this is work that's been conjured out of nowhere just to placate me. If every other firm in the vicinity turned this job down, then I doubt SDC has any expectation of taking it on. Then again, beggars can't be choosers, and I'd rather be doing something, anything, than nothing at all.

Tomorrow I'm going to go to this ruined mansion and document every fucking brick, every stone, every wall. If nothing else, it will keep me occupied and away from the compound for the day. My club should feel like home, but right now, being there makes me feel less than useless.

CHAPTER FOUR
HOUND

Since the accident, I haven't slept well. Even out of the hospital, without nurses checking me every five minutes, I still can't relax and sleep. Last night was no exception. The pains in my leg keep me from being able to find a comfortable position, and there's always a constant dull throb in my head. That fact I keep to myself, not wanting to admit even to myself that I might have a lasting brain injury.

Although unrested, I awake the next morning feeling better than I have for a long while. *I've something to do. A direction to go in.* I'm even polite and refrain from snapping anyone's head off when I go down to the clubhouse and partake of the breakfast Sam and the other old ladies have lovingly prepared.

Stomach full, I head out in the blazing sunlight, putting on sunglasses to shield my eyes and slipping a ball cap on. Then, with more than a tinge of envy, I hop/swing on my crutches as I pass my brothers getting their bikes ready for a ride. Heading on down to the compound entrance, I make my way to the rear of the shop where the club's four-wheel vehicles are stored. With the Arizona weather, most of us use our bikes year-round, and there's not really a reason for any of us to own cages. A few brothers have tricked-out trucks, and most of the old ladies have their own cars, even the ones who have their own motorcycles, due to the need to ferry kids and grandkids around. Like the majority of my brothers, I don't own anything other than my hog, so I appreciate that the club has a couple of SUVs available for anyone's use.

It's my left leg that was shattered, so I have full use of my right. The only problem I have getting into the cage is trying to stow my crutches and then manoeuvring myself to get into the driver's seat with a left leg unable to bear weight or bend.

Sweat appears on my forehead, having achieved the task. I take a couple of moments to catch my breath and use them to check the file I'd been given, then program the address I need into the navigation system. Despite being in a cage, I feel a sense of independence and freedom as I select drive, then make my way out of the compound, heavy metal on the radio turned up loud.

In this day and age, I trust the GPS to guide me, and just obey its instructions without really taking notice of the destination I'm heading to. I'm neither surprised nor disappointed as the road takes me into the foothills of the Catalina Mountains and into a forested area. *Damn.* I must have passed the entrance, as I know I've headed long past where the GPS had told me I'd arrived. I do a convoluted three-point, well, probably closer to a five-point turn on the narrow road, and head back the way I'd come. Driving more slowly, I peer through the trees, and eventually, on my left, see an opening more by luck than anything. Backing up a few feet, I steer the car in that direction, then swear as I come up to a chained and padlocked gate.

The lock doesn't bother me. Shooter had given me a set of keys yesterday, and one is certain to fit. But it's the effort it's going to take to get out of the car, traverse the uneven ground, and open a gate that looks like it hasn't been touched in ages. Undergrowth has grown up around it, entwining itself around the rails and providing a natural deterrent to keep people out.

My optimism that I might not be in the right place fades as I see a broken sign hanging lopsided from a post. *Sullivan House.* It announces exactly where I'm supposed to be.

Shit, fuck and damnation. For a second, I'm tempted to call for help, but I've been enough of a drag on the club recently, unable to do my job or hold my own. This is a task that's been assigned to me, and me only. I'll be damned if I give up at the first hurdle.

I do pause to take a picture of what I'm faced with. After all, Bullet and Shooter had asked for a complete portfolio on the house, and they need to know the lengths I've gone through to satisfy them. *Maybe they'll grovel after the event.* Opening my door, I reverse the process I used to get inside. Crutches under me, I pick my way carefully across the rutted track. Feeling unbalanced and wary of crashing over if my crutch slips into a hole, I approach the gate, momentarily hoping I don't have the right key on the ring I'm carrying. But luck is, or maybe not, on my side, as the padlock opens with a few backward and forward jiggling motions. Not so much the gate, that's stuck, held in place by the greenery.

I start to examine it, wondering if I need to return for a machete to hack my way through, but notice, although voluminous, the individual vines aren't thick. New growth, by the look of it. Recalling the picture I'd seen taken of the house, someone must have passed this way within the past few months or not much more. My knife should be able to handle it.

Which is easier than it sounds balanced on just one leg, and it takes me about three times as long as it would have if I had use of both lower limbs. But eventually I've cleared it, and managed to push the reluctant gate open, which protests the movement with loud creaks.

Now it's back to the car, re-stowing my crutches and situating myself inside, something that takes far more effort than it should.

Minutes later, I'm driving along a paved road that has definitely seen better days. Weeds are numerous, and potholes abound, making me glad the club owns the four-wheel-drive SUV and that it's not in my name. If the suspension gets jacked, then we have the skills to replace it.

The road winds through the low-hanging trees, some lower branches and leaves brushing against the windshield, but I carefully make my way on, slowly, as I don't want to damage the glass. I'm peering ahead when the vegetation clears and the house comes into sight.

House is too informal a name for it. Just like the picture had shown, it's an imposing mansion, the style of which is not common in Arizona, where adobe buildings are more the norm. Sweeping around the weed-covered semi-circular driveway, I pull up at the front door. After staring at the impressive portal in wonder, I get out of the car, crutches supporting me as I try to hold my phone in one hand to take the pictures that will show the state of the building in front of me.

To my amateurish eyes, it looks sound, as if it's survived a couple of hundred years and will live for two hundred more. The frontage is impressive, with columns supporting the elaborate canopy. The double front door, topping the three marble steps, is both welcoming and forbidding at the same time. It feels like a consequential moment as I clamber up the stairs, select the correct key, insert it into the lock and turn it. After a shove and a groan, the door opens to reveal an aged, but still ornate interior. For a second, I almost expect a butler to approach me, to ask for my card and tell me to wait while he goes to find the lady or master of the house.

I chuckle to myself as there's no welcome except for silence, cobwebs and dust. Looking down, I see the black-and-white marble-tiled floor of the central hall, then around to see rooms off to each side. In the centre is a sweeping wooden staircase leading to the second floor. Although divested of most of the furniture and covered with the obvious signs of years of neglect, it still somehow manages to look elegant. I snap a few photos, thinking it would be a shame to tear this place down, while the sensible part of me wonders who, in this day and age, would want to maintain a house of this size in such an isolated spot. Then again, if demolished, what good use could be made of the plot?

The windows are unshuttered. Sunshine, filtered by the trees outside, illuminates my surroundings as I set out to explore. On the first floor, I encounter a reception room, peeling wallpaper, and several gaps in the wood parquet floor that I'm careful to keep my crutches out of. There's a mouldy couch, and two armchairs, so old-fashioned I deduce it's been deserted for a decade or more. Next, I come to a dining room. A huge table that can seat at least a dozen guests dominates the room. Off the hall is also a kitchen, with outdated appliances galore, nothing to salvage, nothing old enough to go into a museum, or sufficiently modern to be sold secondhand. The last room is a library, with shelves upon shelves of musty-smelling books. The kind that I recall being described as "bought by the yard", that is, ones purchased not for their contents, but for appearances, to make the house owner seem learned.

My phone clicks and clicks as I capture each image, wanting Bullet and Shooter to have enough information to make a professional decision on the future of this house. As I survey my surroundings, I feel privileged, as though I'm party to a private tour of a house under the guardianship of a historical society. Stories of the past drip from these walls. I imagine balls in the hallway, spilling out into the reception rooms. Women in elegant long dresses, men in tuxedos. Breathing in, I can almost smell the odour of cigar smoke.

I find only one anomaly on the first floor. During my second visit to the lounge, in the corner, I see a heap of half-burned items. Curtains, if I'm not mistaken. Another sniff in the air, and I'm sure I can sense the lingering hint of gas. *Has someone tried to start a fire here?* Whether deliberate or not, it doesn't seem to have spread too far. There's little to no damage to the structure of the house. Nevertheless, I faithfully use my phone to record the scene.

Having completed my photographic inventory of the first floor, I carefully start my upward ascent of the stairs, testing each step before I put my full weight on it. There are creaks, but nothing major that would suggest the structure is unsound. As I rise, I admire the Palladian windows and dentil mouldings. In its heyday, this place would have been worth a fortune. It's hardly any stretch of the imagination to hear voices and music of people partying downstairs, staff moving unseen between floors, and all kinds of decadent enjoyment. A twenties' ball, celebrations after the First World War, and maybe the second. I'm certain this house holds a myriad of memories if only its walls could talk.

On the second floor, corridors spread out to the right and left of the impressive staircase, and a less elaborate stairway leads to the upper third floor, presumably where the servants spent their time when not attending to their mistresses and masters. I find six impressive bedrooms. Entering the first, I hold tight onto the doorframe, as there's a huge hole in the floor, thanking the gods that I'd proceeded carefully. If I'd fallen through, I'd have undone all the hard work the surgeons had achieved on my left leg and probably damaged my right as well, let alone picking up any other injuries to add to my collection. Checking my phone, I notice I have no signal, so I'd be fucked if I incapacitated myself.

Once my heart rate has returned to normal, I continue to explore. The second bedroom and third bedroom are in about the same state, devoid of all furniture, and the floors look so weak that I hastily retreat. Retracing my footsteps, I return to the staircase and head down the other corridor. The next bedroom here is smaller, empty and bleak, with cobweb-covered glass obscuring the windows.

Feeling hairs rising on the back of my neck, I realise this place is giving me the creeps, and I'm one of the most level-headed guys you could ever meet. I don't follow religion, worship a spiritual being in the sky, or believe there's anything after this one life we're given. Which means there should be no reason at all why I keep looking over my shoulder, or why I'm experiencing the overwhelming feeling that I should get out of here *now*.

I force myself on, ensuring I'm photographing everything, wanting to make sure I capture everything the first time. I'm already starting to feel I never want to come back.

I look into the next room, where magazine cuttings from the 2000s hang on the walls, showing pop stars of the day, suggesting that once a teenager lived here, but there's nothing else to be seen. I take photos but otherwise leave the room as I found it.

The final door on this floor, I hesitate before opening, as if I've some sixth sense of warning. Despite the hairs rising on the back of my neck, I straighten my back, reminding myself that I'm here to do a job. My hand shakes as I press down on the handle, then I can't suppress my gasp. It's a room trapped in time, this time fully furnished, dominated by a four-poster bed, complete with brocade hangings and a mattress. There's a dressing table, adorned with three surround mirrors, with a full set of brushes and combs laid out on top, and a full-height, ornately carved double closet. While the overwhelming smell of decay sweeps in from the corridor behind, here there's a faint lingering odour of perfume. I feel like an intruder as I snap picture after picture, without venturing fully into the room.

Slowly, I become aware that the house is darkening although it's only midday. The light coming in from the windows has diminished to the extent I need to turn on the flashlight on my phone. I leap back as a flash of lightning briefly illuminates my surroundings, followed by a crack of thunder so loud, it has to be right overhead. *It's fucking October. Too late for monsoons.* Must be an errant storm that's blown up. But hell, that was so close I swear I can smell sulphur.

I don't understand my urgent urge to retreat, but I obey it anyway. As I manoeuvre my crutches to take me closer to the stairs, I hear a sudden crack, and a huge beam falls from the ceiling only inches in front of my feet. Frozen, I look up to see flakes of plaster fluttering down.

There's an inner voice screaming inside my skull, *get out, you don't belong here,* and I find myself propelling my body toward the stairwell, only to realise I haven't explored the upper floors.

How could I explain to Shooter and Bullet that I couldn't complete the job because I felt, let's face it, scared? I couldn't. I pull myself together. The beam fell because it was its time. The whole damn property should be condemned, and I'm just here to prove it. I make my way around the hallway back to the upper stairway, then, heart beating like it's going to jump out of my chest, I start to make my way up.

Crash. A rumble of thunder so loud, I'm not sure my eardrums are still intact, accompanied by the roaring of rain hitting the roof.

Then another beam falls, blocking the stairwell.

Now I'm not a suspicious guy, but I'm in an old house at the end of its life, and it's falling down around me. I'm disabled. I can't run. All I can do is limp my way down. I'm not afraid to admit I turn, and as fast as I can, make my way back to the ground floor.

It might be my overactive imagination, but I swear I hear the house groaning, old wood giving way. I don't miss the way the walls seem to be moving, as if they're breathing in and out, and hear words on the wind coming through the broken windows. *"You're not welcome here." "Get out." "Leave before it's too late."*

My heart thumping, breathing laboured, my crutches impeding my progress as I descend each step, I hop/swing my way toward the main doorway. I step out into the open, suddenly realising the sky ahead has cleared and there are no clouds in sight, and no signs of any rainstorm. Even the ground is bone dry.

What the fuck?

Without even a glance back, I go to the SUV, get in and start the engine. My tyres spin as I roar away from that house. I don't stop to close the gate.

CHAPTER FIVE
HOUND

Pressing the pedal to the metal, I don't ease up my speed until I'm far away from the Sullivan House. It's not until I near civilisation that I slow, sufficiently sentient to not want to pick up a ticket. My brain is full of the warnings the doctor gave me about my TBI—hallucinations, seeing shit that's not real, hearing things that aren't there. I reckon I probably look crazy, my lunacy clear on my face. All I need is an overexuberant cop to pick me up and maybe see something in me that says I shouldn't be driving at all.

I don't consider returning to SD Construction to give my report to Bullet and Shooter. Hell, I'm in possession of photographic evidence, but I don't want to review the pictures, too scared my brain might again be playing tricks. I do know I'm in dire need of a drink, and once I start downing the whisky, I doubt I'm going to stop. Heading straight to the compound, I park the car behind the shop, retrieve my crutches, then manage to make my way up the slope and into the clubhouse.

Razza's behind the bar and raises a brow at my approach.

"Whisky, double," I snap, managing to get my ass on the

bar stool. While propping my crutches up alongside me, my trembling hands betray me, and one crashes to the floor.

"Hey, Brother, what gives?" Peg advances, his tall form overshadowing me until he bends, retrieves the crutch, and sets it beside its twin. Brimming with health and fitness, he reminds me of the mess I am. He might be in his sixties, but he still works out in the gym every day, and misses looking his age by a mile. And for now, at least, he's stolen my job.

Glancing at him, hoping soon he'll give it back, though I'm starting to have doubts whether I'll ever again be mentally fit for the role, I morosely reply, "Feel so fuckin' useless, Peg."

"Not that useless," another voice barks. "Heard you've been doing some work down at SD Construction." Widening my eyes as I look toward Drummer, he snorts. "Zeke told me."

Of course, his fucking son told him. Nothing's a secret in this club.

"Would rather be riding my bike and kicking ass." I can't stop the resentment coming out of my mouth. I've downed my first drink. I tap on the bar to get Razza's attention, and request a second double.

"Whoa," Peg warns me. "Better go easy, Hound. You want your leg to heal, and if you fall on your face, you'll undo all the surgeon's good work."

Drummer's sharp, discerning eyes obviously see more than I want him to know. "Wanna talk about it?" he asks.

My experience so recent, and the drink having loosened my tongue, the words escape before I can stop them. "What? That Bullet and Shooter sent me to check out a haunted house?" *Just let the floor open up and swallow me now.* I act fast to cover my misstep. I force a snort as I rush to correct myself. "Well, that's what it felt like. Old building, unoccupied for years, half falling down. Holes in the floors. The place was a disaster, not to say a death trap."

"Why the fuck did they send you there?" Peg growls, slamming his hand on the bar. "You could have injured yourself more than you already have."

Feeling protective of the one business arm of the Satan's Devils that had actually offered me a job, I shrug. "It wasn't that bad. Just had to be careful."

"Sounds creepy as fuck," Drummer responds with a laugh. "You see any ghosts while you were there?"

"Ha fuckin' ha," I reply. "No ghost and no souls, living or departed." I take a large sip of my whisky. "Place looked like the Disney haunted house if you want a comparison."

Looking concerned, Drummer carefully looks into my eyes. "You get any strange feelings or impulses while you were there?" As my face twists to look at him with a total lack of comprehension, he clarifies, "Know you were diagnosed with a TBI, Hound. The wrong stimuli could fuck with your head."

How the fuck does he know? "You been speaking to my doctor?" I rasp out through gritted teeth.

"Wasn't him, Bro. I hacked into your medical records." It's Mouse who's appeared. He shrugs at my glare and raises his hands. "I did it for all of you who were injured. Prez," he inclines his head toward Drummer, "needed to know what we're dealing with and the best way to help."

Wizard's my prez, not Drummer. I scowl. "I'm not fucked in the head. Doctor said it was a possibility, not a certainty."

A meaty hand lands on my shoulder. "Brother, we just want to give you what you need so you can heal." Peg shakes his head. "My ol' lady's looking to retire any day now. I don't want this extra responsibility for a moment longer than I have to. Need you back in the harness."

"But fit and well," Drummer adds.

"I'm well," I growl, then admit, "The fitness I've just got to work on."

"True words. You look like shit, Brother."

"Gee, thanks, Peg," I snarl.

Mouse orders himself a soda, then steps closer. "I looked into the Sullivan House when Bullet asked me to. It's an anomaly in time, left vacant for years. A woman called Siobhan Sullivan inherited it, but it's been nothing more than a mill-stone around her neck. Do you know she actually tried to burn it down?"

Tilting my head to one side, I non-verbally encourage him to say more, the charred remains I'd found. If that was evidence of her arson, she hadn't gotten far.

He doesn't disappoint. "There's nothing to actually say it was her, but someone started a fire in one of the downstairs rooms. Used gasoline by all reports, but the flames just petered out." His eyes meet mine. "She's tried to get it demolished a few times, but every company she approached ran into prob-lems. A man was electrocuted when he tried to send his bull-dozer through the front door. Another had a heart attack just entering the grounds." He shakes his head, and his hair, once jet black but tinged with grey now, settles around his shoul-ders. "SD Construction was this Siobhan's last chance to get something done."

Gobsmacked, I don't know what to say. I'd sensed the house wasn't normal, that something was going on. But right now, with Drummer's reference to my brain injury, I can't admit that to anyone.

His half-Native American heritage showing now, Mouse's pupils widen, and he seems to be meditating for a moment. His hand lands on my arm. "Never doubt your senses, Brother. There are more things in this world than we acknowledge."

Shrugging him off, I sneer, "I wasn't afraid. It was just an old abandoned house. Decaying, and yeah, concerning, as I wasn't sure I was going to make it out of there without the place collapsing around me."

"I'm going to have a word with my fuckin' son," Drummer growls. "You're supposed to be taking care of yourself, not being put in danger."

Hurrying to ease his concern, I try to shed a better light on it. "I'm exaggerating. I just had a close shave that shocked me, is all. I think the house is probably sound, but it's deteriorating on a daily basis through neglect. I doubt Zeke, Bullet or Shooter had any idea of the condition in which I'd found it." I raise and lower my shoulders. "I'm here. I got out. No injuries to body... or *mind*." I emphasise the last word.

Mouse slaps my shoulder and shakes his head. "It's lucky you went there today, and not later this week, Bro. Halloween's approaching," he adds to make sure I understand him. "Any spirits hanging around are bound to come out then." He lifts his hands and wiggles them as though he's imitating a ghost.

Peg snorts with laughter, and Drummer follows suit. "Mouse, you're a laugh a minute, ain't ya?" He points at me. "Better lay off, else you'll get him believing this shit."

Mouse's enigmatic smile gives nothing away.

"Anyway," I tell them. "Got no need to go back again. Got all the pictures I need for Bullet and Shooter to know what state that house is in."

With that, the spotlight is off me. Peg, Drummer and Mouse start to talk about their kids. I politely ask for the latest update on Wizard, who's yet to be released from the hospital. Oh, and I picked up that a woman ran out of the clubhouse after Dollar brought her home, and she didn't feel able to experience his kink. That's the only information that had me smiling that evening. *Fucking Dollar.* Even as an old man, he's still up to his tricks.

"Well, I'm off to see my woman." Drummer's hand lands on my shoulder as he leaves.

Blade, who's just arrived to overhear the end of our conversation, barks a laugh. "Hey, it's Halloween soon. How about we all dress up?" He jumps back as Drummer's fist shoots out.

"You fuckin' wish," he growls, as he raises his chin toward us and leaves.

Blade raises his palms in a *what have I done now* gesture and innocently says, "I meant the kids."

"Sure you did, fucker," Peg responds, adding in a slap around Blade's head for good measure.

It's good to be back. This is what I missed—the camaraderie, the teasing. Slowing my drinking, I keep shooting the shit with my brothers for a while, until Clover, one of the sweet butts, approaches. Peg, Mouse and Blade magically disappear, reminding me I've never once seen them cheat on their old ladies.

As the last man standing, Clover sashays up to me. "Feel like having fun?"

I fucking wish. I know she'd do all the work were I to take her up on her offer, and before I was injured, I'd be one of the first to take advantage of her free pussy. But the thought of her jumping up and down on my shattered leg fills me with horror. The pursuit of regaining full motion in my damaged limb trumps any desire to get my rocks off. "Not tonight, darlin'." I remove her hand from my knee.

Realising it would be pretty stupid to drink myself into a stupor, and undo all the work I've done to facilitate healing, and thereafter regaining my place in the MC, I place my empty glass on the bar, and exit the clubroom.

Balancing myself on the crutches, I make my way up past the blocks which house the suites where the unattached members live, continuing up to the top of the compound, where many of us have built houses. I'd claimed my plot when I'd thought I'd found my one, and when that relationship so quickly came to an end, I'd seen no reason not to continue the build for myself.

I let myself into the four-bedroom home that's admittedly enormous for just me, but far more luxurious than the suites the single brothers use. Placing my cut on the peg just inside the door, installed for that very purpose, I walk through the lounge, passing the kitchen that's rarely used and, after manoeuvring up the stairs, on into the master suite.

Entering the bathroom, I shrug off my clothes and glare at the stool that's been placed in the shower for me.

I suppose I'm lucky I've healed enough to be trusted to wash myself alone. While I'm not particularly bothered about my nudity, it really sucked when I was in the hospital and one of the nurses had always insisted on assisting me. But it still irks that I need to sit where I used to stand proudly.

Once clean, I fall into my bed, hoping for a dreamless sleep. Knowing I can't put off tomorrow, when I have to face up to Bullet and Shooter, and lie about what I've seen.

Wishing for and getting aren't anything close to the main thing. Nightmares haunt me throughout the night, in which I'm trying to move as though through treacle, with some amorphous, but definitely evil figure close on my heels. I wake with a jolt, sweat dampening both my face and the sheet that covers me, feeling as if I'd had no sleep, but with no desire to close my eyes and try again.

It's too damn early, but I force myself out of bed and take another awkward shower using the plastic stool and the shower spray to wash every part of me except for my left leg. Dressing, I choose another pair of baggy jeans that I can just about manage to get over the cast, and the first tee that comes to hand.

Entering the kitchen, I study the almost empty fridge, finding only an open carton of milk. Being a typical bachelor, I normally eat down at the clubhouse rather than cooking for myself, but none of the old ladies will be making up anything at this time of day. Grabbing some cereal out of a cupboard, I tip it into a bowl and, after sniffing to make sure it hasn't gone bad, use the last of the milk. Which now means I can only have black coffee. *Fuck my life.*

Not for the first time, I wonder whether it would have been more sensible to cut down on the scale of my house. Why do I need a fully fitted kitchen when, even with all my functioning limbs, I can't remember ever turning the stove on? The microwave gets more use than anything.

Living alone doesn't bother me, not when just a few strides will take me to one of my brothers' houses, or a couple of hundred yards more will take me down to the clubhouse. Not that anyone will likely be awake at this god-awful hour. Today, though, my house doesn't seem a home to me, the space around me seems wasted, as if something's missing.

I switch on the television, scrolling through the channels until I reach a mind-numbing film I've seen many times before. Nothing else has caught my attention, so I settle down on the sofa, letting my mind drift as there's no need for me to follow the plot.

Unfortunately, my mind wanders to the revelations I'll soon need to make to Bullet and Shooter.

I'd rather never revisit the house, even mentally, by relating everything that I saw. But seeing as I'm currently otherwise a waste of space to my club, I have to pull up my big boy pants and complete the task they'd given me.

CHAPTER SIX
HOUND

As before, I park in the employee's parking lot behind SD Construction, enter the building and take the elevator to the top floor. I've not notified my brothers of the exact time I'll be arriving, but since they are expecting me to report back today, I take a chance that at least one of them will be free. Luckily, Bullet is available, and I'm shown directly into his office.

After giving me a grin and a chin lift, he asks, "What gives, Brother?" He motions me to a chair.

Replying as nonchalantly as I can, I slap my phone down in front of him. "Got those photos that you requested." *And job done*, I think to myself. I can get on with my life and forget the Sullivan House altogether.

Bullet takes my phone, holds it up to my face, then connects it to the computer in front of him. As the pictures take their time to load, to centre myself and avoid too much thought about the images he's going to want to talk about, I ask, "What do you think of the F.O.G.s stepping back up into officer roles?"

Settling back, putting his hands behind his head, Bullet chuckles. "Those oldies have done nothing but cause mischief since they retired. I reckon they're fuckin' bored. The accident gave them the chance to feel useful again."

"What if they decide to step back permanently?" I speak the words before I'm aware that I have expressed my greatest concern. Peg was always a fucking hard act to follow. Deep down inside me, I've always been trying to compete, comparing myself to the man who went before. What if I've not proved good enough, and this is an excuse to replace me? Will the brothers notice the difference and no longer want me? That wouldn't even be a question if, going forward, I'm going to be plagued with a traumatic brain injury. Who'd want a sergeant-at-arms who can't separate fiction from reality?

Bullet barks a laugh. "Brother, I've been in the club forever. Drummer was my prez from the day I prospected. He wouldn't have stepped down if he hadn't thought Wizard was a worthy replacement." He pauses and purses his lips. "Change comes to none of us easily. Have to admit, I was dubious at first, but I gave Wiz a chance as he had Drummer's backing and support." He snorts. "But he's proved a great prez. Different from Drum, but lacking in nothing. I've no issues recognising him as Prez in his own right." He shrugs. "Same with Throttle taking over from Blade, Hawk from Wraith and," he glances up to meet my eyes, "you taking over from Peg. You're all the next generation, a recognition that the club has to move with the times." He holds my gaze. "Right now, Wiz is in a bad way. Hawk, Throttle and you need time to mend. Any other club might have folded or been at the mercy of our enemies. But we've got Drummer, Wraith, Peg and Blade to step up to help and run the club seamlessly. With their reputations, anyone has to think twice about taking advantage of our weakness and coming for us." He breaks off, raises and lowers his shoulders again. "Sure, they're enjoying themselves, but I can't see them thinking of being anything other than caretakers." Chuckling softly, he finishes, "They've all been there, done that. And before the crash, I saw no signs of any of them wanting to hold officer positions again."

Touching my temples, remembering what happened yesterday, and the doctor's ominous warning, I admit, "I worry they're regretting the decision to promote me to officer."

"Fuck no." He looks amazed. "Look, you were in a coma. I attended church during those early days after the accident. If those men hadn't stepped back up, we'd have been floundering. It's not a judgment on you, Brother, it just is what it is." He grins and leans forward, adding confidentially, "They are enjoying themselves, but it's only with the knowledge it's temporary. I'm actually one of the F.O.G.s myself, and once retirement beckons, it's not something you give up voluntarily."

"But you're here," I counter. "Running SD Construction like you always have."

"Different from running the club, but even so, I'm going to be stepping down soon. My heart sort of went out of it when Viper died. And Carmen is going to be giving up her hairdressing business. There's a whole new freedom I'd like to explore. I have confidence Shooter and Zane can run the business. There's no need for me to be here getting in their way." He leans back in his chair. "Know it's hard to believe that power isn't everything. As you get older, things come into perspective. Like wanting more downtime to be with your ol' lady and enjoying life with fewer commitments." His eyes sharpen. "If you're worried about your position in the club, don't be. Hey, I happen to know Darcy's close to retiring, which is all Peg ever wanted her to do. He's always been on edge with her being a firefighter. Once she hangs up her helmet for good,

Peg won't want extra responsibility. He'll want to spend every moment with her."

Feeling more at ease, I adjust the position of my left leg. "Them photos ready yet?"

Bullet snorts, then turns his screen around, so I can watch as he clicks on the file and opens it.

The first shot is one of my leg. The second one of the ground. The third some blurred scenery. He groans. I put my head into my hands. "Fuckin' tell me it gets better than this, Brother."

Shaking my head, I can only hope that it does.

"There was a gate blocking the driveway. Had a little difficulty opening it," I admit, as finally he clicks on an image that makes sense.

"I can see." His eyes widen. "You had to cut through that?"

"Sure did."

"Should have called for help," he remarks, as he steps through to the picture of the gate once it's been opened. His eyes move to my leg encased in metal and plaster, and he shakes his head. "Surprised you even got through."

Whether he's giving me criticism or not, he continues clicking through the photos. He lets out air as he sees the columns and the grand entrance. "The other photos don't do this place justice," he says, and then continues to examine each of the many pictures I've taken. "Fuck, Bro, this house must have been amazing in its day. You've captured everything." He grimaces. "Including the decay. The way the floorboards have fallen in, I'd bet good money dry rot riddles everything."

"It was pretty impressive," I start, but am interrupted by the buzzing of a device on his desk.

He presses a button and snaps impatiently, "What?"

"Think you need to come out here, Bullet." I recognise the voice of his receptionist.

With an apologetic glance toward me, he gets up and leaves. "Give me a minute," he says as he opens the door and disappears.

Alone, I stay still. I'm tempted to go around to the keyboard and click through the rest of the images I captured, but I resist. That fucking mansion unnerved me enough as it is. I don't want to subject myself to remembering the distress, the panic, that an MC sergeant-at-arms, a seasoned Marine to boot, shouldn't have experienced. There was an unseasonal monsoon while I was in the mansion. I heard the rain, saw the lightning, and was almost deafened by the thunder. Yet no sign of it when I came out, and as for the house seeming to come alive around me... the sooner I forget about that the better. I stare down at my hands, watching them shake in my lap, remembering how the doctor warned about my prognosis when he talked about my TBI. Hallucinations could well be part of that.

But what would that mean? If I were seeing and hearing things that weren't there, how could I regain my role as sergeant-at-arms in the club?

The door opens, the sound making me jump. *Fuck, now my nerves are shot.* Looking up, I expect to see Bullet, but he's not alone. I don't recognise the woman who's following him into the room, wondering why he's allowing her to interrupt our meeting. Surprised, I take a moment to examine her. There's something timeless and ageless about her. She could be anything between late twenties to mid-thirties, at my guess. She's dressed in capri pants that show off her shapely legs, some kind of floral shirt covered by a light jacket, a nod to the autumn air. Her face is stunning, with only a hint of makeup enhancing her features, and glossy red hair tumbles down around her shoulders in a mass of curls. Her green eyes and generous freckles suggest the colour is natural. The jacket is open, allowing me to notice a waist so tiny I wouldn't be surprised if I could span it with both of my hands, ample breasts, and, as she turns slightly to take the seat Bullet directs her to, I can't miss the ass that's to die for, pert, round and firm.

Cocking a brow toward Bullet, I wait to be introduced.

"Ms Sullivan," he starts, with a chin lift toward her, "This is Hound, my colleague, who just visited the property you were enquiring about."

"Maeve," she says, in a voice with a tint of an Irish lilt. She sits, but clasps her hands and leans forward. "You went there? To Sullivan House?" Her eyes flare with interest.

For some reason, I have to clear my throat before answering. "Yes," I confirm, managing to repress the shudder that just the name causes.

Her eyes widen as she leans forward. "It's still standing? You went inside?" Her questions tumble out fast.

"Yes," I again answer in the affirmative, concentrating on keeping my voice steady. My hands tremble, so I clasp them over my knees.

Luckily, she shifts her attention to Bullet, who by now has seated himself behind his desk. "I want to see it for myself. Please take me there."

What? Hell no. That place should be bulldozed rather than visited. I interrupt, "Not much to see, darlin'." For some reason, the endearment falls off my tongue. "It's a ruin and far too dangerous to go inside."

Bullet glances at me sharply, his eyes narrowing. A raised eyebrow speaks volumes that I hadn't led with that comment when I'd first entered the room. "Dangerous?"

Shrugging, I try to explain myself. "Holes in the floors. A couple of ceiling beams fell when I was there."

For a second, he looks chagrined. "Fuck, Bro, didn't mean to put you in the way of being hurt."

"All's good," I quickly reassure him. But to her, I say, "It's really not worth going inside."

She looks upset, gutted, and Bullet's not immune. He studies her for a moment, then says, "You're not listed as an owner. Why are you so interested in seeing the house? You looking to buy it?"

She sighs loudly. "My aunt owns it, but I lived there with my Grammy. My mom took me there when she was diagnosed with Stage 4 cancer. When she died, Grammy looked after me from when I was thirteen. I've got so many good memories of that place, I just want to see it again."

"There's not much to see," I tell her. "Sure, there's a bit of furniture still there, but that's no use to anyone, and there were no personal effects that I could see. It's just an empty rotting hulk that will fall down by itself if it's left for much longer."

Biting her lip, she looks from me to Bullet. "You're going to think I'm crazy, but something's calling to me from there. I *need* to go. I know I've no right to demand the keys, but please, let me see where I grew up." Turning to me, she adds, "I'll be careful and heed your warnings." Back to Bullet, she directs, "I'll be happy to sign anything to give you indemnity should anything happen while I'm there. I'll take full responsibility."

Taking pity on her, Bullet looks at his screen, then turns it around. "Hound took photos while he was there. You can look through them with us. It might be enough to satisfy your curiosity."

"Photos?" She brightens a little and sits forward. "I'd like to see them, please."

Always the gentleman, well, with his wife and in business, perhaps not so much with some of the jobs he's been called on to do for the club, Bullet complies. He comes around to the front of his desk, standing between us so he can view them at the same time. Leaning forward, he returns to the beginning, clicking fast through the first few pictures until he gets past the embarrassing ones and my attempts to open the gate. He pauses on the image of the house's exterior.

Her hand covers her mouth to smother a little gasp. "It's been neglected," she concurs. "But it's still the place I grew up."

Slowly, giving her time to savour each picture, he clicks through the shots. Her distress is palpable as she sees the inside of the house, obviously so changed from the happy days when she'd lived there.

As he goes through the copious photos I'd taken, she's shaking her head. He clicks forward, she stills, points her finger at the screen, and demands, "Go back."

Bullet returns to the previous picture. I lean forward to get a better look, trying to see what's caught her attention.

Oh fuck. Oh my God. What the hell? That's the master bedroom for sure, the only room in the house that was fully furnished but... the photographic evidence I'd taken shows that it's not. There's a four-poster bed, but it's leaning precariously. There's no mattress or curtains, and that dressing table that looked like it was just waiting for its mistress to sit and prepare herself for an evening out? Well, it's lying, broken, and upended on the floor. Doors hang off the closet that looks like a breeze would blow it down.

But that's not the worst thing. While the picture indeed shows evidence I'm losing my mind, there, at the back of the casual snap I took, there's a shape of a woman, not quite solid, but undeniably present. I blink, then blink again. *Christ. My TBI must be worse than I thought.* My palms start sweating. *Was I hallucinating then or now?*

Before I can topple down into my own personal rabbit hole of hell, Maeve states firmly in a voice full of wonder, "That's my Grammy."

"Nonsense," Bullet replies with more than a dose of common sense in his voice. "It's a reflection of dust in the light coming in from between the blinds."

The fact that she's seeing what I am pulls me up, and I lean forward for a closer look. Something eclipsing my fear of a major TBI is that there might have been someone else in that house while I was there. As sergeant-at-arms, I should be aware of my surroundings at all times, and I thought I'd developed a sixth sense that would warn me if someone who shouldn't be there was present.

"Is your Grammy still alive?" My question is driven by desperation.

Dashed when she turns her amazing emerald eyes on me, she says, "She died fifteen years ago."

"A trick of the light," Bullet repeats with emphasis, and chuckles. "Cameras don't catch ghosts."

Nor spirit furnishings it seems. I clench my fists.

Maeve sits upright, her spine straight, eyes flashing in challenge. "Whatever. In none of the photos do I see any hazard that I can't be careful to avoid. I want to go there. Will you let me have the keys?"

Bullet shakes his head. "I've got to contact your aunt..."

So far, I'd thought Maeve to be a sweet woman. I've obviously underestimated her as her backbone seems to grow in front of my eyes, as she hisses, "My aunt's got fuck all to do with this. That house is rightfully mine. She stole the inheritance from me." As Bullet opens his mouth, she waves a hand and continues, "Oh, I can't do anything about the will. Grammy died before she could alter it. But I do demand that I go visit that house one last time." After pausing, she adds,

"With or without the keys." She shrugs. "As you say, it's falling down. If I break down the front door, nobody would notice."

Bullet, also taken by surprise at her vehemence, glances at me, a question in his eyes. Then to her, he asks, "I suppose there's no point telling you you'd be trespassing?"

The rigidity of her posture confirms the warning won't have the slightest effect. And, to be honest, even if the Satan's Devils were inclined to call in the law, I doubt the police would take much notice of a house which has been abandoned for years and holds nothing of value. Hell, even a vandal would be hard-pressed to leave it in much worse a state than it already is.

"Ms Sullivan—"

She stands. "I think our business is complete."

Bullet swings around fast. "Wait." She at least pauses, half turned toward the door. He breathes in deeply, then lets air out on a long exhale. "Can't give you the keys. And while they are in our possession, we have responsibility for looking after the property, whatever state it's in." She bristles again, but he follows up fast. "Since I can't stop you, I won't let you go alone. If you're that determined to see the place, Hound will take you."

Her eyes alight with pleasure, while I need to suppress the immediate urge to vomit.

CHAPTER SEVEN

HOUND

No fucking way do I ever want to go back to that house again. I send a silent plea toward Bullet, hoping he'll rethink, reemphasise that while it might have been her residence in the past, she's got no rights to go there now.

To his credit, he does try to dissuade her. "I think you're making a mistake. You've got happy memories of that house, and seeing it in its current state would probably ruin them. Why not remember it how it was?" He purposely circles back to one of the photos showing the huge hole in the floor.

Yes. Mentally, I fist pump the air, unable to remember a time when I actually wanted to kiss a brother. I refrain, of course, but I'm happy he's read my mind.

Her lips thin. "Nevertheless, I want to go back and see for myself."

After examining her for a minute, Bullet sees her determination, and assesses it's not worth trying to change her mind. "Okay then, You'll go with Hound."

What the fuck? Kiss him? Right now, I'd rather kill him.

"No," I say fast, sitting forward to make my point with body language, my sudden action causing my crutches to fall to the ground.

Up to that point, it seems she hadn't noticed my cast-encased leg, as she breathes in sharply. "Of course, you can't go. I didn't realise you, your…" she waves her hand toward me as if trying to find a politically correct way of pointing out I'm disabled, and settles for, "predicament."

Grimacing, Bullet shakes his head in apology. "Sorry, Bro. I forgot. You're right, you need to stay well away from that place." He gives a wry grin. "Both Drummer and Wiz would have my ass if you re-injured yourself."

I tell people what to do. Except for those from my prez and VP, I don't take orders. And if someone tells me I can't do something, I'm genetically disposed to prove them wrong. It's so natural to contradict him, I forget I'm arguing against my better judgment. "I've got a broken leg," I hiss. "I'm not an invalid. I've been there once, I can go back again." I even raise a brow in challenge.

"Hound," he starts patiently.

"No." I slash my hand through the air. "I can do this."

After raising his eyes to the heavens and letting out a sigh, he pronounces, "It appears to be settled then. You'll take Ms. Sullivan to her family home and show her around to satisfy her curiosity."

Fucking hell! Why hadn't I kept my mouth shut? What argument could I now offer as to why he's sending me to a place where usually wild horses wouldn't be able to drive me? Nothing at all, unless I want to admit my doubts about the extent of my brain injury, and that the house had caused me to hallucinate. One mention of a possible mental impairment would see me demoted for far longer than it would take my leg to heal, and give probable cause for my club to doubt my sanity.

"Sure," I say as nonchalantly as possible, while gritting my teeth. I edge to the front of my seat and eye my crutches lying on the floor. Taking pity on me, Bullet leans down, picks them up and passes them to me. His face, turned away from Maeve, shows me a smirk.

Bullet, as one of the older members, has been in the club far longer than I have. While not officially one of the F.O.G.s, he's fucking with me in the same way that they would. He knows I don't want to go back to that house, but he left me no option other than to call his bluff. I'm stuck. I either have to admit fear of the supernatural or confess to a brain injury that might risk everything I've strived for.

Crutches under me, I get to my feet. As I turn, my eyes fall on the flip calendar that's on Bullet's desk. October thirty-first. *It fucking would be.* I wonder whether I should try to persuade her that leaving the visit until tomorrow would be best, but Bullet would haze the fuck out of me, and I can just imagine her look of disdain. I keep quiet.

I've had time to practice this shit, get my supports under me, and try my hardest to make my progress look easy as I lead the way out of the offices of SD Construction, proving to myself and everyone that being on crutches doesn't mean I'm weak. I head toward the SUV, but she stays back. Noticing, I turn and raise a brow.

"I'll follow you in my car."

She's waving toward a cheap rental that's likely to split apart on the road we'll be covering. I snort an incredulous laugh. "No fuckin' way. The driveway to the house has been neglected for years, and unless you've got four-wheel drive and don't give a fuck about your suspension, there's no way you'll be getting to the house." Or, if by some miracle she gets there, I doubt she'd get back.

She looks at me dubiously. "I don't like driving with strangers."

An out at last. Shrugging, I tell her, "Don't give a fuck. You want to see the house, I can take you. You worried about driving with me, then you can just turn around and go back to wherever you came from." Then I remind her, "It was you who came to SD Construction for help."

She bites her lip, drawing my attention to it. *She's got the perfect-shaped mouth to take my dick inside it.* Where that thought came from, I've no idea.

I'm a biker. I'm no virgin. Being inspired by the successful relationships of my brothers in the club, I briefly tried a relationship. Hell of a start to it we had, when I damn near rode into her on my bike. She'd been crossing the road without looking and jumped away just in time, but tripped and landed flat on her face. I'd stopped to check that she was okay, and when I saw her beauty, I thought fate had thrown her into my arms. Turns out looks are one thing, character is another. Bitten and burned, I'd parted company with her and went back to enjoying the sweet butts and hang arounds. There was never any need for me to go without pussy, not with the patch that I wear. There's also no need for my cock to make its interest known, not with this woman who's making me return to that fucking destination.

"Okay," she says, finally, her admission showing her desire to visit the house overrides her caution. *Thank fuck she can't read minds, or see my embarrassment through the baggy apparel I'm wearing. She'd be running in the other direction.* "But," she indicates my leg, "are you okay to drive?"

"Right leg's fine, darlin'. Just get in."

If I weren't handicapped as I am, I'd have opened the

passenger door for her, but it would be a hassle to handle my crutches and balance on my leg. Anyway, given the circumstances, I see no need to prove myself a gentleman.

Leaving her to tend to herself, I go to the driver's side, stow my crutches, and, balancing on my good leg, slide myself in. Once she's settled, I start the engine and pull away.

For a few moments, we drive in silence. Out of the corner of my eye, I see her fidgeting and am not surprised when she starts up a conversation. The topic is predictable.

"What happened to your leg?"

"Bike accident," I reply. "It's gonna heal. May set off alarms if I ever want to fly, though."

"You ride a motorcycle?"

I navigate through Tucson, heading out of the city, before I answer her. "I'm a biker."

"A biker?" She frowns. "You say that like it's a way of life."

Chuckling, I inform her, "It is. I'm a member of the Satan's Devils MC."

I hear the "*oh shit*" murmured under her breath, and see the anxious look she gives to the door handle.

"Hey, you've no need to worry. Didn't you get it? SD Construction? It's the club's company."

"SD? Oh," she breathes out. "No, I thought it was the owner's initials or something."

"Not from around here, are you, darlin'?"

"Not for some years," she confirms.

Strange, I think to myself. The Satan's Devils have been around for decades, and back in Bastard's day they deserved the reputation most people associate with motorcycle clubs. Surely, she'd have heard of us growing up? Or maybe not, if she was sheltered in the huge mansion.

I continue driving, following the route I'd promised myself never to travel again. The conversation has died out with the confirmation of my lifestyle. I don't really know what to say to her, short of suggesting that getting acquainted with my dick is a better idea than visiting her childhood home. Reminding myself that not only am I currently out of action, I'm on Satan's Devils' business and can't let down the club, I keep those thoughts to myself.

Likewise, perhaps disconcerted by my admission that I'm a member of an outlaw club, she keeps quiet.

As we reach our destination, I'm thankful I hadn't closed the gate. My heart rate speeds up as I negotiate the road, apologising for the rattling I'm giving her bones, before pulling up outside the house. I hope I do nothing to embarrass myself, like jumping at shadows. But then remind myself we're here, chasing a ghost she thought she saw in a picture.

No way. There was no one else here. And I don't believe in the supernatural. If I imagined anything, it was a result of my brain injury.

She peers up at the house as I put the car into park. Risking a glance at her, I see her lips are pressed tightly together.

"I warned you. It's been abandoned for years."

"It shouldn't be this way," she almost whispers. "The house should have come to me. I'd have filled it with love and family."

"You're married?"

A quick glance at me, then she says, "No."

Barking a laugh, I tell her, "Then no way would you have been able to afford the upkeep and taxes, unless you're a multi-millionaire." She's dressed smartly, and I might be an ignorant biker, but even I know her clothes aren't designer labels. "Believe me, you're better off without this burden around your neck." Like her, I gaze at the façade. "Your aunt's in a bind. If it's restored, who the fuck would want to buy a property this size nowadays? It's too far out of town, let alone big enough to be turned into a hotel. And if it's bulldozed, then the same thing stands. It's not the kind of area for new-build houses. I've no idea who originally thought it was a good idea to construct a house here."

"My great-grandfather," she says, as if my comment were a question. "He came from the East Coast with the idea of discovering gold. And he did. Then my grandfather inherited, but the gold had run out by then, though he was left a fortune." She pauses, then continues, "My gramma used to tell me when she first came to the house, there were servants, maids, a cook, a gardener, and a butler. But by the time I came along, it was only Gramma here."

I really don't want to go back inside, but there's no point just sitting here prolonging the agony. My pulse rate speeds up just looking at the house. Before I give myself a heart attack, I reach out and open the door. "You wanted to see it, let's go."

It's then that I feel her reluctance, but don't understand why, due to her prior insistence. But maybe, now she's here, she's aware of just how much deterioration has occurred since she last stepped through the front door.

"We can just go back to Tucson," I offer.

"No," she says sharply. "I'm here now. I want the full tour."

Thoughts go through my head, like why didn't I leave my debrief with Bullet until tomorrow? Then he'd have been the one to have to deal with her. Or, why did I chicken out yesterday and return to the club rather than giving him the photos straight away? But I can't go back in time, I'm here now.

She waits while I hop on my right leg to open the back door and extract the crutches, get situated, and then start to move.

There are three steps up to the entrance. I don't miss the pitying glance she sends toward my injured leg, before she asks, "Are you sure you can manage?"

"Don't worry about me," I reply, deliberately trying to make accommodating my leg and crutches look easy. Reaching the top, I twist the key in the lock, but there's no need. The door pushes open. It's then I remember not shutting it properly after I'd run out like the demons of hell were after me. At her incredulous look, I shrug my shoulders sheepishly, knowing she's wondering why we'd made such a fuss about giving her the key.

Perhaps it's because she's so eager to go in, but she lets me off lightly when she could have complained about the unprofessionalism of SD Construction.

Taking advantage of her lack of attention to detail, I open the door. After waving her through in front of me, I step into the hallway that's lit by the golden glow of a sunset, the light casting a halo around Maeve's head. It's picturesque until... *what the fuck?* Ducking my head back around the doorway, I notice the bright sun of an Arizona autumn afternoon.

It must be the effect of the old glass in the windows, I rationalise.

Maeve's just standing, looking around in amazement. Her face is relaxed as if she's really feeling she's coming home. She turns in a circle, holding her hands out, as if taking the atmosphere in. Then she turns and informs me, "There used to be a Georgian card table right there. It had an amazing walnut finish and looked just like a hall table until you swivelled it around, then it folded out showing the green felt. It always fascinated me. And there..." her hand touches mine briefly as she points to a corner. "There stood a grandfather clock. It had a sun and moon display on it, and I loved to just stand and watch it. The bong of the chimes could be heard all over the house." Her face falls. "I guess my aunt sold anything of value."

I suspect she's right. To delay exploring the rest of the

house with her, I buy some time by asking, "So how did you come to live with your gramma?"

She sighs as if the subject is painful. "My grandparents had two daughters, Siobhan and Sian." I already know that her Aunt Siobhan was the one to inherit the house. "My aunt was trouble from the start, according to my mom. My mom was the younger sister. Siobhan had her nose put out of joint when Mom was born. She didn't enjoy sharing her parents, and acted out, ironically proving to be the harder child to raise, meaning Sian, my mom, became the favourite. She excelled at everything a lady should do. Played piano, knew how to behave in polite society, and was the beauty the whole county admired. By contrast, Siobhan was a wild card, lost her virginity to the gardener, but all of that was hushed up. Thinking she might be pregnant, my gramma got her married to Thomas O'Reilly, a local, recently widowed, and childless farmer, just to save face." She grimaces as she looks at me. "I feel sorry for her in some ways. Her life couldn't have been easy. My grandad had died young, years earlier. She was only eighteen. Gramma was old-fashioned and thought there was a stigma to being a single mom. Gramma thought she was doing her best, but as it turned out, Siobhan wasn't in the family way. She remained childless all her life and locked into a loveless marriage."

"What happened to your mom?" I ask.

After breathing in deeply, she answers, "Turns out it wasn't just Siobhan who Gramma needed to worry about. Mom was only twenty when she made her own mistake. She fell in love, not with one of my grandparents' circle, but with a man born on the wrong side of the tracks. A tradesman." Walking forward, she rests her hand on the banister of the stairs, caressing it lovingly. "Dad was a good man. His and my mom's only fault was that they preempted their wedding vows. Then, before I was born, he died in a freak accident. They never had the chance to get married. The wedding bands had been bought, and Dad even had the licence. But those truths didn't matter. Siobhan had a husband. When my mom birthed me six months after my dad died, my aunt had ammunition to use against my mother. She managed to persuade my grandmother that the sister, who had a child born out of wedlock was the black sheep and not her. She was now a respectable married woman. She also embellished the story with lies about drugs and my mom getting pregnant as a result of going to wild parties. She intimated my mom whored herself out to drug dealers to fund a nonexistent habit.

"When Mom tried to bring me home, Siobhan's poison turned Gramma against her, resulting in Gramma disowning my mother. Mom was distraught, but sucked it up when Gramma turned her back on her and made her own way in life." Her face lightens. "Mom was resourceful. She'd let nothing beat her. And my dad's parents did what they could to help out." As if I have any doubts, she reassures me, "I was loved by my mother and grandparents. I couldn't have wished for more growing up. But Gramps and Gran died from monoxide poisoning from a faulty gas boiler. Soon after that, Mom was diagnosed with cancer. In grief at the loss of her in-laws, she'd left it too long to get her symptoms checked out, and when they discovered the tumour, she didn't have much time left." I reach out my hand to touch hers, but she shrugs my comfort off. "Mom brought me back here. She and Gramma reconciled and Gramma took us in. Mom had hung on to the marriage licence. Belatedly, Gramma realised how good a man my father had been, and that Siobhan had filled her head with lies. As Siobhan had no children, I was the only grandchild. When my mom passed away, Gramma assured me I'd always be looked after. In her original will, she'd disowned my mother, but she emphatically told me she'd written a new one, which left everything to me."

After listening to her for so long, it takes a moment for me to understand what she's saying. "But the will Bullet's working to, listed your aunt as the beneficiary."

Maeve shrugs. "I can only assume she never actually got around to renewing her will."

Or her aunt destroyed the new one, I think to myself.

"I don't care about the money," she states. "I'd have been happy with just something to remember my grandmother by. In the end, she was so good to me." She gestures around her. "But it looks like everything's gone."

Something strikes me as strange. "Your gramma died fifteen years ago, yet now is the first time you've come back?"

"It was time," she says, succinctly. "Let's move on." Knowing the house, it's she who leads me first into the kitchen, then the dining room, and then the main reception room of the house. Any furniture remaining, she rests her hands on momentarily. "Nothing of significance is left." She sighs as she returns to the hall and eyes the stairs.

While it should still be at its zenith, it's as if the sun is disappearing beneath the horizon. It's starting to get dark in this house that's been abandoned for years. I already know no electricity is connected. It feels ominous, even worse than before, when she places her foot on the first step. Acknowledging my hesitancy but mistaking the reason, she gestures again toward my walking aids. "You don't need to come with me."

"I can make it," I growl, not wanting to admit my reluctance is due to my apprehension, rather than my skill at climbing stairs.

She pauses at the top, then after eyeing cautiously, then stepping over a fallen bean, she indicates a room, and then proceeds toward it. "This was mine, where I stayed." Opening the door, she's surprised, but I'm resigned when we find the area is stripped of all furnishings and bare, just as it was before. Only a few teenage posters remain.

Stepping forward, she opens a closet built into a wall, one I'd ignored. Bending down, she picks something up off the floor. It's a worn teddy bear with moth-eaten ears. She clutches it to her.

"Yours?" I ask, completely unnecessarily.

"Mine," she confirms after a short pause.

I want to question her further, like ask her why she left it behind, but then realise how many memories there are in this house for her. No wonder she's acting strange. She's suffered so much pain, so much hurt, I don't want to pry deeper.

We exit her old bedroom, and she hesitates before going to another door, with her hand on the doorknob. Her voice drops to a whisper. "This was my gramma's room. The place where you took the photo that showed her shape."

"It was a trick of the light," I remind her. "I saw no one here. Maeve, I'm sorry, but your gramma's gone, sweetheart."

"I know," she replies sadly. "Nevertheless, I want to see her room. When I was overwhelmed that my mom was dying, she used to sneak me in here, letting me sleep with her, reminding me I was loved and safe. If anything remains of her, I want to know."

There are no ghosts in this house. Any fragment I might have imagined is a result of my TBI. Nevertheless, I'm more than reluctant for her to open that door. The image in the photo we saw in Bullet's office must have been nothing more than dust disturbed after lying for a decade and a half, swirling up to resemble a shape.

However I try to rationalise it, I'm loath to investigate further. "We can leave now," I tell her. "No shame, no foul.

There won't be anything in there that you want to remember. Everything will be decaying."

Ignoring my warning, she twists the knob. "I need to see for myself."

The light in the house has darkened while we've been talking. Although I know in reality it's still a few hours from sunset, in here, it seems like a different time zone. I can barely see the hall behind me, and when she pushes open the door, it's to see a room lit by flickering candles and oil lamps.

She freezes, and I immediately put my arms around her, pulling her in close to keep her safe.

"What the fuck are you doing?" she yells, jumping back so fast, for a second, I struggle to get my balance.

"What? Protecting you…"

"Protecting me from what?"

I just point to the room behind the open door. "From…" My voice trails off. Here, the light of the setting sun is streaming in through the windows. The flickering I attributed to candles is only the golden rays filtered through the autumn leaves on the trees. The oil lamp? Well, that's the reflection of the sun itself on a trio of mirrors lying forlorn on the floor.

Oh my God! My head spins as the implications flood through me. Sinking to the floor, my plastered leg shoots out in front of me, leaving me to land heavily and undignified, and painfully, on my ass, eliciting a groan of pain to escape my lips.

"Hound! What the hell's happened to you?" Suddenly, Maeve's on her knees by my side, offering a hand to help me up, which is a joke as I probably outweigh her by one hundred pounds.

Even under extreme torture, I could give no excuse for the following words to come out of my mouth. "In the accident where I broke my leg, I had a concussion. I was in a coma for three weeks." Her hand covers her mouth as she gasps. "Doctors warned me that as a result of a traumatic brain injury, I might start acting irrationally, or, like, you know, see things which aren't there."

"Oh, Hound." Her hand now hovers above me. "I wouldn't have wanted you to come here if I'd known." That's quickly followed by her asking me sharply, "And what things are you seeing?"

"I grabbed you as I thought the room was lit by candles and oil lamps." Snorting, I continue, "But it was just the reflection of the sunset."

As I wait to hear her reaction to the thought she's here with a lunatic who can't control himself, I didn't expect her to bite her lip and apologise. "I'm so sorry I pushed you." She tries to put her arm around me to help me up for the second time. "Let's get out of this house."

Leaning on my own arm mostly, I let her believe she's helping me off the floor. When I'm standing on my good leg, she passes me my crutches, and I get them back under me. While all I want to do is escape, I don't want to let her down. "We're here now. May as well finish what we came for."

"And risk you putting your arms around me again?"

Turning fast, I see her grinning at me. Then she shrugs. "You startled me, but I don't mind admitting, I wouldn't feel too bad if that happened again." Her eyes widen as if she's surprised herself with those words. Then, rather than back-tracking as I expect, her cheeks flush as she adds breathily, "I mean, it's not every day I'm in an embrace with a handsome man."

A smirk comes to my face. Of course, I'm not blind to my god-given attributes, but for some reason, knowing Maeve's attracted to me affects me more than any club whore brushing up against my dick and blatantly offering her body for sexual favours. For a moment, it makes me forget my brain injury, and the worrying symptoms I'm experiencing.

Feeling bold, knowing my attraction toward her is reciprocated, I ask, "If you like my arms around you, darlin', how would you feel about a kiss?"

There's only a second's hesitation, before she's rising on her toes, and lifting her face to mine. So much shorter than me, I need to bend to accommodate her, but instead of immediately lowering my lips, I inhale as her warm, and faintly sweet breath mingles with mine. The air seems to crackle with electricity as my eyes narrow to focus on the curve of her mouth, the subtle tilt of her head, and the anticipation in her eyes. I might be reading too much into her expression, but there's a slight quiver to her chin, which makes me wonder if she thinks she's going to disappoint.

Take this slow, I tell myself. She's no club whore offering herself up on a platter—though, in that event, I'd hardly delay things with a kiss. Finally, reverently, I arch my neck, letting our lips meet. Her mouth touches mine, hesitantly before pulling away. It's a testing brush that sends a shiver down my spine. It's hard to say who moves first to find that connection again. This time she stays, allowing me to feel her soft lips, warm, pliant and alive. Finding the small of her back with one hand, I draw her in, tasting something that's somehow more intoxicating that any spirit I've ever imbibed. Blood rushes south, my cock immediately hardening.

Her scent surrounds me as she moans into my mouth, her arms clasping me to her. Her breasts easily felt against my t-shirt make me wish we were naked, and I could see and touch the whole of her body. The air is filled with a faint trace of perfume that I already know is uniquely her. I deepen the kiss, making it slower, more deliberate, more sensual, loving the way she responds. My heart's beating fast, not in fear, but with such an arousal I can't remember ever having felt before. Her little mewls entice me, I forget where I am, who I am, and maybe even my name if I was asked.

Without anything other than tactile communication, our kiss becomes a wordless conversation, each applying pressure then releasing as if in a choreographed dance. Never before have I felt such a magnetic connection.

The house groans as it settles around us, bolting me back into the present, reminding me I'm here to do a job, not to seduce a client. Which she is, whether she's the one paying us or not. My loyalty to my club brothers comes into my mind like a physical slap around the head. Pulling back, slowly, so as not to disappoint her, I pause, plastering just one more sedate caress against her mouth. But the lingering warmth on my lips comes with the quiet ache to feel hers again.

As she steps back, I can't miss her expression that suggests for her, I've just hung the moon. And you know what? I don't fucking hate it. Even with the girl I'd thought was my forever, I've never felt such an immediate and deep connection.

Before I say *fuck it* and act on the invitation that's clearly there, I clear my throat, force a businesslike expression on my face, while taking her hand in mine—a tactile gesture to minimise her disappointment—and step into the room that was once her grandmother's personal domain.

CHAPTER EIGHT
HOUND

Together, we step forward into her gramma's bedroom, and I take a moment to check everything is exactly how I left it before. But of course, it's nothing like how I last saw it with my own eyes. Instead, the room's exactly as the photos foretold. The unstable frame of a four-poster bed remains, still in the same state, with no mattress and no curtains. The dressing table, I'd already noted, is opposite the bed, still lying upturned on the floor, and that wardrobe has doors hanging off, looking abandoned and forlorn. The once majestic wallpaper is peeling off the walls.

Fucking TBI. I close my eyes briefly, swallowing down the panic of what that will mean for my future. Somehow, the hand I still clasp seems to ground me, keeping me in the here and now rather than losing myself in my fear of what lies ahead.

I even centre myself enough to realise that this decay is not how she would have wanted to remember her grandmother. I squeeze her fingers and hold tighter.

"Hound?" she asks, her voice tremulous and urgent.

It was only a moment I was lost in my head, but her tone gets my attention. She's looking behind her, and as I turn, I can see what's gotten her distressed. There's a black vapour rising up the stairs.

Fire? But breathing in, I can smell no smoke, and there's no crackling to suggest flames have taken hold. While being trapped upstairs as the house burns would be dangerous, what panics me more is that there's a shape to the blackness, and the way it swirls shows deliberate intent.

A shiver of fear goes through me. *Is she seeing what I am? If she is... if she's sharing these sights and sounds, then this isn't just my hallucination, this is hers.* She's certainly scared by something. Her eyes are wide, her breaths are close together, her pulse racing when I clasp my hand to her wrist. As the blackness continues to swallow what's behind us, I throw caution and my doubts about my sanity to the wind as I clump my way back to the door and slam it shut. On hearing a loud gasp, I turn back around.

Gramma's bedroom looks completely different, transformed just as it had been last time I was here. Sumptuous velvet curtains surround the four-poster bed, and there's an inviting-looking mattress on it, covered in colourful bedclothes. The peeling wallpaper I'd observed just moments before is now fully restored and looking luxurious.

But it's not the furnishings that capture my attention. It's the couple who've suddenly appeared. She's lithe, stunningly beautiful, looking like she's somewhere in her late twenties, wearing a dress covered in peacock feathers, headdress to match, and he, considerably older in age, in a smart, tailored tuxedo. As they move close, despite the age difference, it's impossible to miss the love shining out of their eyes.

The man, as if entranced by the woman, steps forward,

holding on to her upper arms. "Emerald, my love, my darling. I can't believe it. That you are here, that you are now mine." Reverently, he lifts her left hand, exposing the glistening wedding band on it, and kisses her fingers.

Emerald sighs deeply, placing her right hand over her heart. "Oh, Bertie. You can't know how happy I am. I still can't believe that you saw me, saw the woman beneath the charade, while others looked right through me. I'm the luckiest woman in the world that you took me away from the club."

"Never doubt yourself," he growls. "I might not have been the one to build this mansion, but seeing you here, I know it was made for you, and only you. You were always worth so much more. Others might have denigrated you for your choice of career, but I know you had no alternative. You were only dancing at that club as a way to support yourself." Pulling her to him, he surrounds her with his arms. "No matter how many others' eyes were upon you, you were mine from the moment I saw you, and will be until the end of time."

"I'm yours," she half-whispers in response. "Will you pinch me? I feel like I'm living my best dream, and that I'll wake up in a moment and know it's not real."

Bertie chuckles. "It's as real as it can be. We're married. My ring on your finger proves it." He rubs the hand he's still holding. "You can't escape now."

A soft tinkling laugh comes from her. "The last thing I want to do is run. I love you so much." She casts a look down at the sparkling diamonds on her finger, twisting the ring as if to confirm it's there. "And this house? Bertie Sullivan, I adore everything about it."

"Emerald Sullivan, I love you." His eyes flare, and his mouth tightens. Then, in a gruff voice, he tells her, "And now I'm going to take you for the first time in our house."

Gently, he places his hands on her shoulders and turns her

around, his fingers going to the buttons fastening her dress at her back. Slowly, tortuously, he unbuttons them one by one until the gossamer material and attached features fall to the floor. He spins her back to face his front, giving me a ringside view of her corset, boned and tight, high panties, a suspender belt, and silk stockings covering her legs.

Emerald gasps, leaning forward, placing her cheek to his shoulder, and wrapping an arm around his neck.

Oh fuck no. Sure, I've been a voyeur on numerous occasions, single brothers and sweet butts aren't shy in our club. And I'm also guilty of taking more than one of the whores in public, but that's exactly what they signed up for. But watching what can't be anything other than ghosts getting their freak on? Nah, there's no way I ever signed up for this. As for Maeve, the last thing she wants to see is her gramma, as that's who I'm assuming this is, get fucked by her grandad.

I know I need to get her out of here, but when I try to step away, I'm unable to move, my feet solid as though they're cemented to the spot. Worse, as the couple approaches the bed, they seem to walk straight through us. *Is Maeve sharing my illusions, or has time and space frozen only for me?* I can't even glance her way to check.

I feel no fear, only discomfort that I'm present at the prelude to such an intimate moment. The air shimmers, and now I'm facing the other direction, a direct view of the couple standing by the mattress. I sense Maeve is still beside me, but I'm unable to reach out my hand to give her support, nor turn my head to see whether she's disgusted, upset, or whatever her emotions are, seeing her ancestors about to get their kink on. Both of us are a trapped audience, whether we want to be or not.

Emerald now gets into the action, putting her hands on his

chest and starting to undo the buttons of his shirt. The expression of love in her eyes cuts me to the core. "You were the only one who saw me, who knew what I was and was not."

"You are a treasure." His hands smooth back her hair as he stares lovingly into her eyes. "The way you danced entranced me. Always in peacock feathers."

"Because they matched my eyes." She gives a gentle smile.

He presses a finger over her lips. "I know you say that I saved you from that life, but the truth is, you're the one who saved me." He throws back his head, then looks down once again with a grimace on his face. "You were never a whore, I knew that. You were a woman who had to do what she had to do to get by. Well, damn those who look down on me for marrying the most beautiful woman in the world."

"Your friends think you're crazy." She chuckles.

He grins salaciously. "They can think what they want. I'm the one who got the prize."

"I love you so much," Emerald assures him. While the cynic in me thinks, considering his retelling of her past, she may well have latched on to any man willing to pull her out of the pit she'd fallen into, her breathy tone has me almost believing her. Anyway, Bertie might not have gotten the bad end of the bargain. She sure makes good arm candy. Personally, I reckon his friends might well be jealous that he gets to call her his.

"Damn, baby, I love you so much." Bertie's eyes glaze as he focuses on her.

"I can't believe we're together, here in the house."

Chuckling softly, he replies, "Wel we are. And now I want to claim you as mine in every possible way that a man can." Impatient, he doesn't wait for her to slide all the buttons out of the holes. He rips his shirt apart, sending a scattering of what are probably pearls all over the floor.

His breathing has sped up, his pupils enlarged, his eyes blazing lust.

Oh hell. I'm no prude, but I feel like I'm intruding on something intimate, a first mating of a new husband and wife. I'd give anything to get out of here.

She places her hand against his now naked chest. "You've already done so much for me." She gives a little laugh, comprised of musical tinkling notes. "The men and women who looked down on me will all be begging for invites to our soirées now."

"Where you'll win them over," he tells her.

Again, her tone is full of mirth. "Because you've given me respectability."

Clearly impatient and done with the conversation, he turns her around and starts undoing the laces of her corset. As the garment loosens, she crosses her arms over her chest. She's facing me, so I've a front-row seat to see the hint of uncertainty in her eyes, her voice tremulous. "Go slow, Bertie. I've never done this before."

Like fuck, she hasn't, I think with a slight grin. *Poor Bertie, she's probably pulled a blinder on you.*

Seems I'm not the only one who doubts her as Bertie pulls her to him, cradling her head. "Em, I don't care if I'm the first or hundredth man to have you, I just want to be your last. I'll make it good for you, baby. I promise."

Their lips meet and meld. The kiss, which starts off gentle and romantic, quickly evolves into something more. He ravishes her mouth, and while there's a good part of me that thinks Emerald knew a good thing when she saw him and trapped him, I'm almost convinced she's not faking it when she moans and all but attacks him back. The air seems to sizzle around them, and while it's quite inappropriate, my own cock perks up, interested as if I'm watching porn.

I wish I were anywhere but here. I don't want to be aroused by two ghosts getting it on. I try to close my eyes, but even that seems beyond me.

As their mouths mash together, his arms go around her back. She may not be the professed virgin she told him, but he's obviously no innocent himself. I have to admire his technique. He has no problem edging her out of that corset until it falls loose. He moves his body back without breaking the kiss and lets the garment fall to the floor. The marks left by the tight clothing mar her skin, but he appears not to notice, too enthralled by feeling her now free breasts in his hands.

"You're beautiful," he tells her.

Is that virginal type shudder of apprehension genuine or faked? It's hard to tell. But I can admire a good actor when I see one.

After applying attention to her nipples and tits, his hands move lower and start to pull her panties down, leaving her in a suspender belt and stockings just like I would. Fuck, at this moment, I wish I could move so I could palm my dick as her only slightly trimmed bush is revealed, hinting at what lies underneath.

Funnily, normally, my broken leg would start to protest if I'd been left standing on it so long, but there's no discomfort at all. It's as if I'm being supported by a cloud. But I'm given no time to ponder this as Bertie strips all his clothes off fast, then lifts Emerald in his arms and gently situates her on the bed.

"I'm going to claim my wife now."

Frowning, I watch on in horror as he neither lowers his mouth nor even applies his fingers to get her ready for him. I suppose in their days, sex was all for him, and not for her. I stiffen as I watch him simply push his not inconsiderable cock in, and wince as she tenses and screams. Her reaction isn't faked. The tears leaking from her eyes are genuine.

"Fuck," he says, tensing, then pulling out. As he looks down to see the evidence, I can also clearly see the blood on his dick. "I'm so sorry, sweetheart."

I notice she can barely look at him. I want to scream out, to give him pointers. *Touch her clit for fuck's sake, even if you don't know how to find her G-spot.* It's no wonder men are thought of as animals with just carnal instinct.

"Finish it," Emerald gasps.

With gritted teeth, Bertie pushes himself back in. His pace quickens. I watch her. Fuck, I've heard about just lying back and taking it, but it's clear she just wants it over with.

Never, ever, even with a club whore have I been so unfeeling.

He grunts, thrusts once more, then stills. After a moment, he leans down, kisses her, and tells her how beautiful she is, that she's all he ever wanted. That he hopes his seed took root, and how they could be parents soon.

Then, to my astonishment, Emerald takes his hand and directs it to her clit. "I may be innocent, but I've listened to a lot of people and know about my body. Make me feel good too."

To my surprise, I realise Maeve's moved in front of me, her back against my chest, and in a demanding fashion, she grabs hold of my hand and presses it against her groin. We both watch as Bertie's eyes widen as he flexes his fingers over Emerald's sensitive nub. He grins when he sees her body's reaction and does it again. Kudos to him, but he's a quick learner. And so am I. Cock throbbing, my hands suddenly loosen from the inertia that had enthralled me. I undo the zip of Maeve's pants, feeling how wet she is, and copy Bertie's actions as he changes his movements, starting to strum, and redoubling his efforts when Emerald throws her head back and her muscles tense. When her orgasm floods over her, I'm not quite sure who's most surprised, her or him. But I don't have a moment to think about it, as Maeve tenses, leans into me, then I feel her let go with a scream. As I continue a practised motion of my fingers, prolonging her pleasure before bringing her down, something loosens inside of me, sharing the experience with Bertie as if our minds have become one. Knowing he's going to want to hear Emerald make those sounds, to see her make that expression again and again. *As that's exactly how I feel about Maeve.*

Maeve's still panting heavily as I hold her against me, my cock pulsating, wondering how I'm going to get a release. But my eyes are still transfixed on the scene in front of us.

When their heavy breathing starts to slow, Bertie puts his weight first on his hands, then lifts himself off the bed. Naked as the day he was born, he strides across the room, deflated cock swinging without giving a damn. He heads for the ornate dressing table, pulls out a drawer, then fiddles with something underneath, opening a secret compartment. He pulls out what's within and, with it hidden in his hands, returns to the bed.

"Emerald," he breathes out. "I'd hoped for, desired, the gift that you'd given me. If you hadn't been pure, I'd have given you these on the birth of our first child. But tonight..." his voice sounds choked. "Tonight you've given me more than I've ever dreamed of, so the time is now."

With those words, he fastens an incredible gold and emerald necklace around her neck, places emerald earrings in her ears, a bracelet around her wrist, and tops it by putting a ring on her right hand.

His voice chokes. "I love you so much, Em."

It's so touching, tears prick at the back of my hardened biker eyes. Even though my earlier desire was to get the fuck out of here, as the scene starts fading in front of me, like a movie I've enjoyed every minute of, I now want to continue to watch everything play out. The candles snuff out as though a breeze had blown through, and the oil lamps fade and die. The dim light of the setting sun is the only thing illuminating the room as feeling returns to my legs, the ache of standing too long. I lose my balance and start to fall backward, reaching out for support, which leads me to take Maeve by the arm. Both of us topple over to land not on the bed covered in a soft mattress, but on an unforgiving, hardwood frame that cracks as we land on it, but luckily holds.

"Fuck!" I exclaim as the air's forced out of me. Then, remembering my companion and my manners, ask, "Are you alright?"

I find a soft woman's body rolled on top of me, her mouth finding mine, pressing frantically against my lips. My cock is hard from the scene I'd just witnessed. Her actions lead me to presume that she's equally turned on. Placing my hand around the back of her neck, I pull her lips more firmly down, only to find I'm kissing my own palm, and a whisper lingering in the air... *find me.*

What the fuck?

I sit up, but there's no woman in my arms. The room is empty, a decaying hulk of what was once wondrous and fine.

Have I imagined everything?

There's no lingering perfume, no odour to suggest candles have been recently burned. Just empty air and silence, and absolutely nothing to suggest there was ever anyone else here.

"Fuck no!" I shout, my words echoing around the empty house.

I couldn't have imagined everything. My senses are still tingling with all the visions that, if I close my eyes, I can still touch and feel.

What the fuck is happening?

Find Maeve. She must be around here somewhere. Though Emerald and Bertie might have been ghosts, she was a flesh-and-blood woman. She couldn't simply disappear. Pulling myself up, I slide to my ass, landing hard on the floor by the bed, crawl to the crutches that had been discarded, gather them up, and get them under my arms. My whole body trembles as I limp out into the hallway. I feel weak and lightheaded as I get to the stairs. On the first step, I falter, on the second, I lose my balance and tumble down...

CHAPTER NINE
HOUND

There's a weight on my chest, holding me down, so heavy I feel like I'm suffocating, unable to breathe. My hands feel useless, and my feet can find no purchase beneath me as the ground is like quicksand holding me prisoner. My fingers inadequately claw at the sides of what feels like a bottomless pit. Ineffectively, I struggle to reach the top, falling back down on my first attempt, also my second, and then, the third. Panic gives me strength as I redouble my efforts. I've no idea where I am, just know my life depends on getting out. Another attempt, then one more. I try to swallow my panic, concentrating all my efforts on climbing the walls and escaping whatever's dragging me down. One last deep breath, one final push and endeavour, and my efforts are rewarded as I reach the surface.

Immediately, bright light burns my eyes, and my ears pick up a beeping sound I know only too well from when I was in the hospital a few weeks back. As my sight begins to focus, blinking eyes bring anxious faces into view.

Bullet's the first man whose voice I recognise. "I'm so

fuckin' sorry, Brother. I thought I was helping, sending you to that house. But you clearly weren't ready, and you overdid it." He shakes his head sadly. Then, slightly hopeful, he adds, "Did you actually go? Or weren't you up to it?"

House. Maeve. That he might think I ignored his request and didn't return to the house is overshadowed as I start to recall everything that happened in that cursed Sullivan House. As it comes back to me, I rapidly try to put the pieces together, my experiences replaying like a film in my mind. Finally, it all comes together. "You found me at the bottom of the stairs?" I'm so grateful he thought to come looking for me. Fuck knows what would have happened if no one had come searching. "How long was I lying there?" *And what further damage have I done?* Fuck. All I can remember is flying through the air. I could have shattered my leg even more.

"Stairs?" Now it's Drummer's gruff bark. "What the fuck are you talking about? We found you unconscious just outside your house. Couldn't rouse you, so we had you brought to the hospital."

"Drummer," the softer tones of his woman, Sam's, voice butts in. "He's only just woken up. Go easy on him now."

I shake my head but quickly stop as a blast of pain hammers through my skull. I focus on Bullet. "I went back to the house with Maeve..."

"Maeve?" Bullet asks, his eyes widening. "Who the fuck is that?"

"You know," I spit out, annoyed. "When I came to your office to go over the photos of the Sullivan House, she turned up..."

After giving a worried look toward Drummer, he rolls his eyes. "Brother, you never came back to the office. And I certainly never met anyone called Maeve."

Drummer's arm has gone around his old lady, and his

sharp eyes have softened. "Hound, Brother, looks like you might have left the hospital too soon, and are doing too much. From the way I found you, your crutch must have slipped out from under you, and you went down with a crash. Knocked yourself out again." One side of his mouth turns up. "Sure sounds like you have one fuck of an imagination to dream up shit like that."

What the fuck?

My panicked eyes go to Bullet, a silent plea for clarification. "Earlier today, you came to my office and agreed to go to the Sullivan House." He shrugs. "Don't know rightly, can't say whether you did or not, but whatever you got up to after leaving SD Construction must have been too much. This evening, Drummer found you." He jerks his head toward the acting prez. "As Drummer said, just outside your house at the compound."

No. Fuck no. I look from the concerned faces of Drummer and Sam, to Bullet, whose eyes are tight, then Peg, standing, his brow furrowed behind them. *It was all real. The pornographic scene that I watched with Maeve, the woman I held in my arms, who I brought to orgasm. Maeve, the woman who disappeared into thin air.* I open my mouth to protest, to tell them everything that happened, then realise if they think it was all in my head, then it probably was. Even if it wasn't, if I started to tell my story now, it would only confirm that my brain was fucked. I'd never regain the trust of the club.

Swallowing hard, I come up with an acceptable excuse. "I must have had one fuck of a nightmare."

"Don't worry," Drummer speaks soothingly, in a voice I recall him using when Eli and Zane were children. "We'll fight this with you, Hound. Doc says you didn't damage your leg when you fell, and there's no indication you badly hit your head. Seems you simply passed out. The scans showed no new brain bleeds. Your fall and your confusion are a result of your brain injury. It might only be temporary. Doc says you just need rest to let both your body and brain heal as well as they can."

It doesn't surprise me Drum got the full rundown from my doctor. Even the Hippocratic oath doesn't stand up against one of his death stares. And rest be damned. I'll time out when I'm dead.

Then another thought enters my mind. *They're fucking with me.* There's nothing wrong with my head. I glower at Bullet, wondering why he's lying. I went back to his office, showed him the photos, met Maeve, and reluctantly returned to the house. Where I was met with an X-rated scene, and the woman in my arms evaporated. *Or did I?*

Sure, the F.O.G.s play jokes, but none that would mean me ending up in a hospital bed. Pranks, yes, but cruelty, making me think I'm fucked in the head? I'm sufficiently Copus mentis not to accuse them of that.

Metaphorically zipping my lips firmly shut, I make no more mention of photos, Maeve, or my return visit to the house. I'd be locked up somewhere for my own safety if I kept insisting it was all real.

My visitors shuffle awkwardly, as if unsure of what to say. "What day is it?" I finally ask.

"It's early morning, October twenty-nine," Peg enlightens me, lighting up a little at a question that's easy to answer. "You'd stumbled out of your house and collapsed on the ground late last night."

But that can't be. It had been Halloween already when I returned with Maeve to the house. What the fuck is going on? I couldn't have hallucinated everything. Could I? If I did, my brain is more fucked than I thought. Goosebumps rise on my body as a chill goes through me, feeling like icy blood flowing through my veins.

"The doctors want to keep you in for observation for a while. Do a few tests, make sure there's nothing they've missed," Drummer informs me. He pats my hand gently. "All you've got to do is rest and get well again."

I'd already felt well, mentally, that is. I know my leg is still healing. I'm reeling from being back in the hospital again. Everything I've gone through feels so real. I can't believe it was all a dream.

"Get some rest, Brother." Bullet, too, sounds concerned as he gets up to leave.

"Maeve," I croak out. "Maeve Sullivan. Get Mouse to look into her, please?"

"Sure, we will," Peg placates me, placing his hand over mine. "Just concentrate on yourself for now, Brother. Get some sleep."

After what happened the last time I closed my eyes, I'm not sure I ever want to sleep again. Even with all the evidence against it, I can't believe the whole thing's been a dream. That I never left the compound, never showed Bullet my photos, never met Maeve. Never revisited the Sullivan House. But it all seemed so real. Maybe I'm living in an alternate reality.

Alone, my heartbeat increases. I seem to be jumping from one time to another, and neither of which I want to be the truth. Which would I rather? To accept my brain is totally fucked, or to believe that, after witnessing a porn scene between ghosts, the woman I was with evaporated in my arms. Notwithstanding, I seem to have lived a day that didn't yet exist.

Seeing as it's hard as fuck to get any rest in a hospital, with nurses coming in and out to check you're still breathing and other vitals, and trolleys rattling up and down the corridors outside, I don't get a chance to drift into the deep sleep that I'd need to be in to dream. Early afternoon, I'm not rested at all, but at least I think I have my sanity about me.

Lucky, because it's the consultant who's been treating me who's first up. Without niceties, he gets straight down to business. "You remember what caused you to black out?"

I have no recollection. Well, that's not true. I recall clearly toppling down the stairs in the Sullivan House. But to explain how my brothers found me collapsed outside my own home, I've no idea. I'm also intelligent enough to know there would be implications if I told the doctor that I didn't know how I came to lose consciousness. I give him the words that I think he needs. "Fuckin' crutches got caught on something. I went down hard. Obviously knocked the wind and senses out of me."

He smiles and nods, as if I'm a child who has passed a test. Then, he informs me, "Your latest scans show no new brain bleeds or swelling on your brain. You clearly didn't do yourself more damage." I already know that. Drummer had told me. I acknowledge his words with a chin lift. After staring at me for a moment, he adds, "If you fell and knocked your head, that's one thing. But if for no reason you blacked out, then that would be far more serious. I'd have to recommend you stop driving."

Fuck no. It's bad enough not being able to ride my bike, and while I hate being confined to a cage, I'd go totally mad if I lost my independence completely. "I fell," I try to reassure him. "I'll be more careful."

"Mr Ockenden, may I remind you that you could suffer a number of effects after the serious injury to your brain? You could have seizures. It's important that you're honest and truthful, as more people than just yourself could be injured or killed if you're trying to hide your symptoms."

I don't know what the fuck happened. I think one thing, my club tells me another. The truth lies somewhere in between. While I get what he's saying, I refuse to believe I'm a danger to anyone other than myself.

"I tripped, I fell," I tell him again. Not really a lie, I just hadn't done it where my brothers thought I did. Or maybe I had. Fuck knows.

He sighs. "Okay, I'll get the paperwork signed off, and you're free to go home."

Left alone, I'm lost in my head, visions of Maeve filling my mind. But if my brothers are to be believed, she's someone I've never met. And, if I had delusions, she never existed except in my dreams. *So why can I still smell the perfume that surrounded her? Why do I still feel the touch of her in my arms?* Fuck having this blow to my head, I've no idea what's real.

How can you feel the loss of something you've never had?

I suppose it must be guilt, thinking he pushed me too far, that has Bullet being the one to arrive to give me a lift back to the compound. The hospital demands I'm taken out in a wheelchair, although I stand on my one working leg and use crutches as soon as I can. Waving off Bullet's help, I get myself into the truck.

On the way back to the compound, he tries to apologise again. "Brother, I'm sorry. I didn't realise you needed to rest."

"Fuck that, Bullet," I respond. "I went to the house and got the job done." Remembering that going over the photos in his office was only something that had happened in my head, I add, "I went to the house, took the pictures you requested. I'll get them to you so you can assess the state of the place for yourself."

"For fuck's sake, Hound." He slams his hand on the steering wheel. "I'm driving you home from the fuckin' hospital. There's no rush, no hurry—"

"I'm fine." I put all the strength that I can into my voice. "It wasn't what you asked me to do that caused me to pass out." It was going back the second time, but, of course, I don't mention that. "I went, I saw, and I'm fit to report back."

"Appreciate that, Hound." He gives a cautious glance toward me before returning his attention to the road. "I shouldn't push, but I'm interested. What was your assessment?"

Place needs to be burned to the ground. Realising probably nothing I experienced was other than visions built up in my mind, I give him the answer I think will bear up. "Not too much structural damage, but the place is a wreck. In my uneducated opinion, it would be better to knock it down. I suppose it could be restored, but who the fuck would want to buy a fuckin' mansion like that? It's too far out of town to be turned into a hotel, and the same goes for anyone wanting to build new houses there."

He gifts me a glance that looks like he's impressed. "Hear you loud and clear, Bro. I'll look at the snaps you've taken. My gut feeling is that you're right. Restored? Who would buy it? Build new? Same question applies. I'm starting to understand why no other construction companies wanted to take the job on."

Thank fuck some of my thoughts make sense.

The rest of the ride back to the compound is undertaken in silence. When we arrive, Bullet sends me a questioning glance to determine whether he should drive me up to my house or park the truck behind the shop as usual. Pride wins out as I indicate I can take it from here. It's my own fault that I'm faced with the long slog with my crutches and busted leg.

When he tries to offer help, I shrug him off, put a swing into my crutch-supported hop, and, trying to ignore the way he hovers behind me, make my way past the clubhouse, the suites, and finally reach my house at the top of the compound. My door's not locked. What's the point when there's only Satan's Devils on the compound? I push it open and step in.

I'm greeted by the aroma of cooking, and Sam, Drummer's woman, Sophie, whose old man is Wraith, Becca, who's Rock's, and Blade's Tash, all invading my kitchen. I suppress my annoyance as I'm actually hungry as fuck—hospital food sucks. I do notice my home is now spotless, discarded clothes laundered and put away, dust collected, and the weeks-old, tied-off condoms from my *before-the-accident* liaisons with sweet butts thrown in the trash.

"Welcome home!" Sam declares when she turns and spots me. "Come, sit, we've got chili and garlic bread ready to go." She ushers me to a stool at my kitchen counter.

"Do you ever cook here?" Tash asks, as she loads up a plate with rice and smothers it with the amazing-smelling chili. "This kitchen's a dream, but all the appliances look brand new."

They would be. Although I've actually lived here for a few years, the kitchen was fitted out to cater to the needs of the woman who I'd thought would be my ride or die. Unfortunately, the one I'd found proved to be anything but. While I probably could put something together to feed myself, I've been too lazy, preferring to eat what the old ladies cook up in the clubhouse. *What would Maeve make of my kitchen?* Fuck. Why did that thought come into my head? *Maeve doesn't exist.*

Before I answer, I take a forkful of the chili and place it in my mouth. It tastes as good as it smells. Waving my fork in the air, I explain, "Never can be bothered to cook something for myself."

"Too damn lazy." Sophie snorts, but softens her words with a wink.

The annoyance at the invasion of my house fades as I eat

the delicious food. Watching my brothers' old ladies clean up after themselves, I realise I'll be left full and with no kitchen to tidy up.

"How are you feeling?" Becca asks, pulling up another stool to sit opposite me.

My mouth full of meat and rice, I don't immediately answer. I take a moment to recall the stories about how she, before my time, came here unable to say boo to the proverbial goose, how she'd been schooled from childhood to defer to everyone, and ended up being abused because of the man her parents basically sold her to. Rock had discovered her when he went undercover for the Satan's Devils. With his support, and that of everyone in the club, she'd found her own voice.

Now I'm looking at a comfortable, assertive woman, and I give her the respect she deserves. Having swallowed my food, I answer truthfully, "Like I've been kicked in the head."

"Crutches are the devil's invention." Sophie laughs, pausing to give me a pat on the arm. "I can't tell you how many times I tripped and fell on my face when I was learning to walk again."

I appreciate her sympathy, but my case is different. She lost a limb. I'll one day get mine back in working order. But at least they're all buying my story, that I knocked myself out having mis-stepped.

"How are the others doing?" I'm fed up with being the topic of conversation.

Sam beams. "Wizard's going to be home any day now. He'll be in a wheelchair for a while, but the doctors are predicting a full recovery. Hawk and Throttle are like you, just having to wait a while longer for their bones to mend." She rests her hand on my shoulder. "Won't be too long, Hound, before you and your brothers are riding again and heading the club, and

Drummer, Peg, Blade and Wraith can go back to being the annoying fuckin' old guys."

Sophie almost chokes as she laughs, and I raise my brows.

Sam grins widely. "Yeah, we all know what you call them. Myself, I'd probably say they were pains in the ass." While Tash almost doubles up laughing, Drummer's old lady continues, "Tell you what, Hound. Once you're able to ride, you can race me around Road's track. I might even give you a chance to beat me."

Narrowing my eyes, I point a finger at her. "You can try."

Road, a brother who used to ride with the Tucson brothers, has been in Utah for over two decades now. He used to be a competitive trial bike rider until he was involved in a serious crash. Before that, the club had used his hobby to cover up a multitude of bodies they'd had to get rid of by creating a practice track through the woods and burying the evidence underneath. Over the years, the track's been extended for the original reasons. I wish I'd been there the first time they'd tried it out, as I've heard numerous stories about it—each brother riding Road's trial bike and trying to make the fastest time. All while Road had to watch and grimace, being injured, and just a prospect then, unable to protest. Legend goes that Sam had taken her turn last and had ridden every other rider's time into dust. She's kept up the record ever since, but now that she's issued that challenge, I'm determined to beat her. She might not know it, but she's given me a goal to aim for.

When they are eventually satisfied that I'm fed and have everything I need to look after myself, the old ladies leave. It's only when the door closes behind them that all my worries come tumbling back.

What the fuck is going on? My mind says I visited Bullet, showed him the photos I'd taken of the Sullivan House, that Maeve had come to his office, and that I'd taken her back to the house. What happened there still replays in my head in full technicolour. Yet evidence suggests I never left the compound, and lost my footing and collapsed outside of my home, while I clearly remember Maeve disappearing into thin air, and me crashing down the stairs.

Fuck! Maeve disappearing. Of course, my brain is fucked to shit. That couldn't have happened. My brothers have to be right. It never did. *Am I actually going mad?* My hands tremble when I hold them in front of me. *Why am I so convinced I've seen and experienced things that couldn't ever have happened?* All of a sudden, I'm so fucking scared. The doctor's warnings had wafted over my head when I'd heard them, but what if this is my life from now on? Seeing and hearing things, living stories that are only fiction to everyone else? At risk of passing out?

Fuck it. I lower my head into my hands. Sure, Sam can be confident that Wizard, Throttle and Hawk will soon be fit enough to resume their officer roles. But what if I end up being a liability to the club because of my brain injury? Who'd want someone who couldn't separate reality from nightmares and dreams?

As it is, I can count myself lucky. For now, the evidence was in my favour. The doctor I'd seen in the hospital had accepted I had fallen and probably banged my head for a second time. If the truth came out that I had a blackout while suffering delusions, I'd no longer be deemed safe to drive, let alone ride. As for those hallucinations? I'd be lucky not to be carted off as a risk to the safety of others.

If I can't ride, I can't be part of the club.

I'd rather eat a bullet than be unable to be a Devil.

And if my brain can't be trusted, maybe that's the only solution.

CHAPTER TEN
HOUND

After the old ladies have gone, I stay in my house alone. If I went to the clubhouse, I'd be smothered with people watching my every move and questioning my health and the state of my mind. I did invent an imaginary timeline and fictional woman after all. The main problem is that, despite evidence to the contrary, I can't believe my version isn't real. *Perhaps I'm dreaming now?* But rubbing my overfilled stomach, I have to admit that's as far-fetched as the alternate reality my mind had conjured.

Finally, the hands on the clock tick around sufficiently to warrant me going to bed. I toss and turn for a while before dropping off into a, thankfully, dreamless sleep. I'm woken abruptly, not by a nonexistent vision, but by the insistence of the ringing of my phone, which threatens to vibrate its way off the bedside table. Groaning and turning, I reach over to pick the annoying device up, noting it's ten a.m. *Shit. I've overslept.* Something I never do, and something else, I suppose, I can put down to my brain injury.

"Hi, Bullet," I answer, seeing his name on the screen, trying to keep my voice even so as not to betray the anxiety in my head. "What can I do for you?"

"How are you feeling today, Bro?"

Doubts about my sanity aside, my head's no longer pounding, I'm not lying when I respond, "I'm good. What can I do for you?"

"Was just wondering whether you could give your phone to one of the prospects so we can see the pictures you took of the Sullivan House?"

"No need to bother a prospect. I'll bring them to your office myself."

Bullet sounds doubtful. "You sure you're up to it?"

Giving myself a fist bump, I remember to stick to their story. "Yeah. I'll be careful on my crutches leaving the house."

"You better be, Bro," he snarls, but in a joking tone. "Don't want to be visiting you in the hospital again."

And there's no way I want to go back to that place either. "Give me an hour and I'll be there."

As I work around my crutches, I shower and dress in shorts I can easily get over my cast, then put on a black t-shirt. I spare a moment to look longingly at my cut. I resist the urge to feel its comforting weight settling over my shoulders. Not only will I have to remove it before I get into the cage, there are doubts in my head that I'll ever deserve to wear it again.

Then I give myself a mental pep talk. The only way forward is to believe I'd stepped into an elaborate dream world, and to accept everything I'd thought happened yesterday had all been a figment of my imagination. Not the original visit to the Sullivan House, the very pictures he was referring to are proof of that. But everything that happened afterward, including meeting Maeve, returning to the mansion, and the kinky ghosts. When I'd fallen and knocked myself out, the only reasonable way to move on was to believe what happened afterward must have been conjured up by my subconscious, despite the overwhelming feeling it was all real.

Pulling back my shoulders, I'm determined to visit Bullet, reiterate my amateur evaluation, and show him the evidence that the house should be demolished. Better still, be burned to the ground. Then I'll walk out, mission accomplished. Simple. Even for a brain-damaged biker.

Making my way down the compound, I again take one of the club's SUVs and head to Tucson, parking at SD Construction.

Shaking off the feelings of déjà vu, I walk into the offices and make my way to Bullet and Shooter's domain. Once again, it's just Bullet who greets me. *Didn't this already happen?*

After a narrowed-eyed assessment, I obviously pass some non-verbal test. "Come on in, Brother." He motions me to a chair. "Sit."

Before I do, I slap my phone down in front of him. "Brought the photos that you requested." I then make my way to the seat, leaning my crutches against the desk. *Haven't I done this before?*

Bullet takes my phone, holds it up to my face, then connects it to the computer in front of him. As the pictures take their time to load, I force myself to stay quiet. My memory, playing tricks on me, replays a whole conversation I'd had with him before. I refuse to ask the same questions, not so much worried I'd get the same reply, but not wanting to tempt history to repeat itself.

It's not history, I remind myself. *I had a vivid dream, nothing real, nothing concrete.*

The air hangs heavy around us, as if anticipating a conversation that goes unsaid. I had vivid memories of me voicing doubts about my future position in the club, and Bullet refuting them. But at least, in this, history doesn't resurrect, and we wait in silence. *In my dream,* I remind myself, *I'd be sat here haunted by memories of going into that fucking house, terrified of reliving the memories.* At least today, I'm not so worried about the tricks the place had played on my mind. But one thing's for certain. Hallucinations or not, I won't ever be going back.

Anticipation reaches its limit, and I adjust the position of my left leg. "Them photos ready yet?"

Bullet snorts, then turns his screen around, so I can watch as he clicks on the file and opens it. Again, the sense of having been here before hits me, but I'm stuck, unable to do anything but go with the flow as I recognise the first shot is one of my leg. The second one of the ground. The third of some blurred scenery. He groans, and I put my head into my hands.

"Fuckin' tell me it gets better than this, Brother."

Shaking my head, I now know that I can. But my mouth opens automatically, and the same words come out that I know I've voiced before.

"There was a gate blocking the track. Had a little difficulty opening it," I admit, as he finally clicks on an image that makes sense.

"Can see that." His eyes widen. "You had to cut through that?"

"Sure did."

"Should have called for help," he remarks as he steps through to the picture of the gate opened. His eyes move to my leg encased in metal and plaster, and he shakes his head. "Surprised you even got through."

Whether he's giving me criticism or not, he continues clicking through the photos. I try to remind myself that I haven't seen them since I viewed them through the camera on my phone, but all the scenes are disturbingly familiar, and so are his reactions—the way he lets out air through his teeth as he sees the columns and the grand entrance. "The original snapshot provided by the owner didn't do this place justice," he says, and then continues to examine each of the many photos I've taken. "Fuck, Bro, this house must have been amazing in its day. You've captured everything." He grimaces. "Including the decay. The way the floorboards have fallen in, I'd bet good money dry rot riddles everything."

I can't stop my eyes from going to the door, waiting to be interrupted, and for Maeve to appear. As Bullet goes through the photos for a second time, time ticks by, still the door remains closed, and there's no visitor.

My heart pounds, my head aches, and I rub at my temples as, finally, I have to admit that everything I'd thought happened was just a dream, all made up in my mind. *Fucking TBI.*

Eventually, the door opens. I look up in anticipation, but it's not Bullet's assistant introducing the literal woman of my dreams. It's Shooter who walks in with Zane following, both of them laughing.

"Hound, my man." Zane grins at me, walking forward with his hand held up. He clasps mine tightly and lifts his chin. "Fuckin' good to see you again."

"Brother." Shooter greets me next, squeezing my shoulder as he walks around the desk to where Bullet has all my masterpieces printed and laid out. Then, remembering I was back in the hospital yesterday, he looks a little cowed and sends me a sheepish look. "Sorry, I should have asked how you are?"

"Fine and fuckin' dandy," I respond, then lie, "Just got my crutch caught on something, fell and banged my head on the ground. No damage done." I stick to the story Drummer had told me.

"Damage was probably done when your mom dropped you on your head as a kid."

I show him my finger but enjoy the banter. It's normal,

recognisable, understandable, and right at this moment, that's exactly what I need.

"These the pics you took of the Sullivan House?" Zane steps forward, his head tilted toward me, so I nod. He responds with a chin lift, then stands next to Shooter, and both peer at the photos Bullet has fanned out.

"You did a good job." Shooter gives me a look that shows he's impressed. "You went in every room?"

"Everywhere," I confirm. "Except for the attic. I didn't want to risk those stairs."

Acknowledging my comment, he tilts his head to the side. "What was your overall impression?"

I'm no architect, designer or builder, but the experts are asking me my opinion. After my brow creases for a moment, trying to stop the words like, haunted, inhabited by ghosts, and fucking terrifying coming out of my mouth, I force myself to sound as casual as possible. "It's been abandoned for a long time. I wouldn't be able to say if it was structurally sound, but as you can see, there was mould and decay all around. Holes in the floors, walls, and ceilings." As they give my words weight and treat me like I know more of what I'm talking about than I do, I continue, "The house must have been magnificent in its day. Easy to imagine high-society parties taking place. But, it's way out in the middle of nowhere." Even I feel I'm now making sense, so in a stronger voice, I give them more. "Some of the glass in the windows was broken, but that's only where trees have overgrown and damaged the frame. What did strike me was the majority of windows were still intact, and the front door closed, no sign that anyone had been there—no kids, thieves, or anyone wanting shelter for the night." As they give considered chin lifts showing their appreciation of my assessment, I give my summation. "Which makes me think a house that size, off the radar, wouldn't be likely to have a market for it if it was restored, or not unless you wanted to live off the grid, and had a fuckload of servants to keep house.”

“Restoration would cost a fortune,” Zane states, picking up a few pictures to examine them more closely. “As would be trying to convert it into apartments. Hound’s right, in that locality, who’d want to live there anyway? It’s way out of town, and the roads aren’t good.”

“I wonder why it’s never burned down,” Shooter muses. “There’s been wildfires in the area over the years, and there’s no firebreak I can see. The trees grow right up to the house.”

The Satan’s Devils are well acquainted with wildfires. Fortunately for us, one burned down the vacation resort that was to become our compound, allowing us to get the land cheap. Long before my time, but the story’s well-known. And then, years later, another burned in the same direction and threatened the compound itself. It had been touch-and-go for a time. That must have been frightening for the brothers in the club at the time. I recall Peg saying his old lady, Darcy, had been one of the front-line firefighters.

“There was evidence…” reaching forward, I shuffle through the pictures until I find the one I want, “that a fire was set inside at some point. It wasn’t successful, and only minor damage done.”

“Deliberate? Insurance job?”

Shrugging, I shake my head. “Couldn’t tell. There was no handy gas can left lying around, but I wouldn’t be surprised. As I said, even pristine, that place would be hard pushed to find a buyer.”

“Unless it was someone who wanted a place off-grid,” Bullet muses.

Shooter punches him lightly in his arm. “SD Construction is legit, Bro. If we take this job on, we’re not going to be courting criminals.”

We all snort. Sure, most of our businesses are above board nowadays, but it's a fine line we walk, and not always the right side of the law. If we did, there would have been no need for Road's track to have been extended as many times as it had.

Zane straightens, his hands going to the middle of his back. He arches as though he's been leaning over a drafting bench for a while. "You'll be dealing with the client, Bullet, but I think the only service we can offer is demolition. And I've fuck all idea what to do with the land."

Shooter nods. "It's easy to see why no one else wanted to take it on. I agree with Zane. Not worth restoring, so we raze it to the ground."

I gather my crutches toward me. "It's in your hands now. I'll leave you to break the news to the owner."

"Siobhan O'Reilly isn't going to be happy." Bullet sighs.

His words have me almost losing my balance and crashing back down. Zane notices my wobble and is there by my side, his hand supporting me until I get myself situated, and my crutches under me once more. I simply thank him and turn my back on the room before they can read the confusion and dismay that must be written all over my face.

Siobhan and Sian, daughters of Emerald, I didn't know who owned the place until I had those conversations with Maeve. *O'Reilly.* That was the name of the man Maeve told me Siobhan had been forced to marry.

No, no, no, and no. Bullet or Shooter must have let it slip the last time I was here. I am not going to let my brain give credence to information from a ghost.

I've got to get out of here. Get back on my home turf and drink myself into a stupor. Alone, in my house, of course, where I can imbibe with no risk of falling down and not be tricked into becoming loose-lipped and giving any insight into what has to be my diseased mind.

CHAPTER ELEVEN

HOUND

It's a miracle I don't crash as I make the drive from downtown Tucson back to the compound. My mind might be fucked, but thankfully, it still seems to work on autopilot. As it is, I'm asking the question, *how did I get here?* while parking the SUV with the rest of the cages behind the auto shop.

Rather than getting out, I stay seated in the vehicle for a moment, head resting on the steering wheel, my heart still beating overtime. *Nothing makes sense.* If I'm hallucinating things that aren't real, then how the hell did I know the full name of the woman who owned the Sullivan House? Shivers run down my spine as I wonder whether I've once again imagined the whole outing to SD Construction, or, at least, made up yet another conversation with Bullet that didn't take place.

Raising my head, I hold my hands out in front of me, noticing the tremble I'm unable to stop. It's coming to the point where I think I should commit myself to an asylum and swap my cut for a straitjacket to prevent becoming a danger to anyone else.

What's happening to me?

Too chicken to seek medical advice as I'm too scared to hear answers I already know, I decide it would be better to self-medicate, drink so much I'm unable to think anymore.

Decision made, I open the door, hop out, pull my crutches to me, then start making my way up the slope. The smell of oil and gas coming from the shop as I pass mingle with the scent of warm desert air flurrying around me. Casting my eye to the left to the edge of our boundary, I see the saguaro and scrub bordering wide open country. I let my eyes roam further toward the foothills and then the mountains. My senses of the very place I call home have a comforting effect, and at last, my heart rate starts to slow. *Maybe I should just impose a personal lockdown on myself. Never leave, never have to face the outside world again.* It's a tempting idea.

Continuing my forward motion, I reach the clubhouse, coming to the row of bikes outside, pausing momentarily, wishing mine was among them, but knowing it's still in the shop. Blade has assured me once my leg's healed, my bike will be whole, and in his words, better than it ever was. I don't doubt him. He's a brilliant mechanic, although with his arthritic hands, he's now got more of a supervisory role. I shake my head. My bike might heal, but I've doubts I ever will.

But as the familiar smells and sounds of ticking, cooling engines roll over me, it reminds me of who I wish I could be. Not the disabled invalid but Hound, a Marine, and sergeant-at-arms of the Satan's Devils, where the club is my life, each brother one I would have no hesitation dying for. Not a property inspector, and not the man who sees ghosts.

Starting to walk again, or taking a step on my good leg, I swing my bad leg in motion, ignoring the clubhouse. I carry on up to my home, open the front door, and walk straight in.

Although I've calmed slightly, that drink still beckons to

me. I head for the cupboard where my liquor is stored. Dismissing the shot glass, I grab the bottle by the neck, unscrew the top, and take a few long swigs. The liquid causes a comforting burn in my throat, so I raise the drink to my mouth to take more, oblivion sounding better by the moment.

I'm interrupted by a knock at my front door. *Damn them.* For a moment I wonder whether I can pretend I'm not in, but good manners win out.

"Come in," I snarl. Turning my head, I see Mouse. Confused, I wonder why this particular brother is here. I beckon him over, and being sociable, wave my hand in the general direction of the kitchen. "There's soda in the fridge." Mouse never drinks alcohol, something to do with him being half-Native American.

"Peg said he saw you walking past the clubhouse." After his explanation of how he knew I was home, he narrows his dark brown eyes and watches me carefully. "You doing okay, Brother?"

I'm past lying. I wave my hand in a see-saw gesture. "I'm getting there."

He eyes the bottle in my hand, but not judgmentally, more as if he's assessing my state of mind.

"What do you need?" I ask, wondering again why he's here. He's the club's computer guru, though he's first to admit, his student and brother-in-law, Wizard, has overtaken him in technical skills.

He grimaces. "You apparently asked me to look into a woman named Maeve Sullivan." He raises an eyebrow.

My forehead scrunches. Hell, everything is so fucked up in my brain. I can't seem to figure out timelines, but that was before I knew I must have dreamed up everything about the woman I'd apparently never met.

I let a loud sigh escape me. "Sorry, that must have sent you on a wild goose chase." I shift awkwardly, embarrassed about having asked him to look for a woman who existed only in my fucked-up head.

"Not at all." He looks at me sharply.

What? It wasn't a fool's errand? Shaking my head, I dismiss the thought. *I imagined her, imagined everything.* Still, I can't stop myself from asking, "She exists?"

"For now," he replies, enigmatically. Mouse looks at me quizzically. Guessing he's got more to say, I beckon him to carry on. He obliges. "Maeve Sullivan is currently at the hospital in Tucson, the same one where you were treated."

My mouth opens and shuts, unsure what to take from this, but he hasn't finished.

"Her car was rammed off the road, coincidentally at the same time as you and the others came off your bikes. Other end of Tucson, though."

Either it's the drink or my sudden euphoria that has my head buzzing. *She could have discharged herself, gone to SD Construction, and accompanied me to the house...*But that would mean Bullet had been lying or forgetful, and neither option adds up. Then Mouse adds something more, which sends my spirits tumbling back down.

"She's been in a coma since that night. Odds seem against her waking up."

I rub hard at my temples. If what Mouse says is true, Maeve couldn't have been a flesh-and-blood woman I took on a tour around the Sullivan House. Not my Maeve, who I held as we watched the erotic scene in front of us. It wasn't my Maeve, who disappeared on me, causing me to panic and fall down the stairs. There's no way unless, unbeknownst to the medical staff, she'd woken up, exited the hospital, then returned to her bed. None of this makes any sense.

"Why the fuck are you doing this to me?" I suddenly roar,

throwing the bottle so it smashes against the far wall. There's another, this time vodka, next to where the whisky had been on the shelf. I pick that up and swig it straight down.

"What the fuck, Hound?" Mouse lurches toward me and takes the bottle out of my hand. "What have I said?"

In my haste to get up, I've knocked my crutches onto the floor. I'm unable to get up to wrestle Mouse for my vodka without them, so I just flail my hands. "What have you said? Too much, too fuckin' little. Mouse, get out."

"Not leaving you like this, Brother." His eyes carry a wealth of concern. "Speak to me."

"And tell you what?" I yell. Like a baby, tears leak from my eyes. "That I'm going mad?"

His eyes narrow. "You're as sane as I am. Now tell me what the fuck's going on."

"I can't." I sound like a petulant child.

He leans back in his seat, crosses his feet at the ankles, and folds his arms. "I'm not going anywhere. Speak to me, Hound."

"I need more vodka first."

Getting up, he passes the bottle to me but takes it back when I've had a few swallows. "Talk," he instructs.

When he again focuses his sharp eyes on me, I feel myself start to fold. Won't be long before all the brothers notice there's something wrong with me and strip me of my role. Might as well come clean, then he can laugh and share the joke with them all.

"I think I've seen a ghost." My voice comes out as a whisper.

As Mouse leans forward, his long hair circles around his face, and he pushes the strands back behind his ears before saying, seriously, "Think or did?" There's no judgment, no laughter. Just pure interest.

How the fuck do I answer that? If I say, I did, he'd think I was crazy, but is just thinking about it any better? I'm hoping like hell, even if my hallucinations are a result of my traumatic brain injury, that just like the bones in my leg, in time, it will heal. There's no need to get brothers looking at me oddly or thinking I can't be trusted in the sergeant-at-arms role.

My mouth opens and shuts, probably making me look like a gaping fish as I wish I could withdraw my earlier statement. Now it's out in the open, I don't know how the fuck I want to deal with it.

Mouse's dark eyes stare into me so intensely, I have to look away.

"Hound," he says in an almost hypnotic tone. "Listen to me. You know my heritage?" I know some of it, but I can't summon up a reply, so he answers his own question. "I'm mixed race, Anglo and Navajo. Spent most of my childhood here in Tucson, enjoying the Anglo lifestyle. I had game consoles, played football, ate fast food, and was a typical teenage boy. Then my dad died, and I returned to the reservation with my mom." He chuckles softly. "Fuck, you can bet I rebelled against it. It was like going back to the Stone Age, but slowly the place took hold of me, seeped into my bones until I acknowledged my Native roots, and along with that, some of the beliefs of the tribe my mom was born into." He pauses, comes and kneels in front of me, then places his hand on my chin, forcing my head to face him. "Hound, listen to me. I learned that most stories had a basis in truth and saw enough to realise there are things that we can't explain, living on the edge of our consciousness. Some spirits are only too real and frighten even me."

"Spirits?" I hang on his word, then think he must be fucking with me, getting me to admit to what I've seen, then share a joke about it with the rest of the club. *Old Hound is losing his mind. You'll never guess what he just told me.*

But there's no mirth in his eyes, and he remains totally serious as he retakes his seat. "It wasn't easy melding the Anglo and Native parts of me. I had to find a way to live with them both. Once I met Mariana and we had the kids, I became more settled. But prior to that, and before you came to the club, I used to disappear for months on vision quests. You know what they are?"

All I can do is shake my head.

"It's where I had let the Navajo part of me take me over, tapped into my spiritual side, felt the world wash away from me as I let the spirits in." He chuckles softly. "Some people would say I was mad, but the club gave me the time, knew I needed to ground myself every now and again." He sighs. "I still get back to the reservation from time to time, but once I was married, my wife and family were all that I needed to ground me. But, Hound, I've seen things no white man would ever understand. If you think you've seen a ghost, believe me, I'm not the one to mock you or disagree." He shudders, and I swear I see goosebumps rise on his arms. "*Yee naaldlooshi*, skin-walkers. Like my tribe, I swear that they're real."

He's not mocking me. The opposite, he's opening up in ways that give me ammunition to turn the tables and make fun of him. But I don't. "I need coffee."

As I start to reach for my crutches, he stops me. "I've got it."

I take the time while he's in my kitchen to analyse his words. *I'm going crazy keeping this all to myself. But can I really trust him?* I study the man, answer him automatically when he asks how I want my drink doctored, and consider how he's always been a steady member of the club—an established fixture long before I joined. Though other brothers aren't against having a joke at someone else's expense, Mouse has never started shit that I can recall. I may be doing him a disservice to doubt his sincerity.

Weighing my options in my mind, I either consider he's a brother who won't let me down or laugh at the preposterous nature of the story I could relate to him, or I can politely tell him everything's alright, see him go, and continue suffering in lonely, tortured silence.

Feeling I've got no choice, first I ask, "What day is it?"

"October thirtieth," he responds, with an eyebrow raised.

"Groundhog day."

He snorts. "Not as far as I know. Care to expand?"

Drawing in a deep breath, I shudder as I let it out. "You're not going to believe this."

"Try me." After passing me my coffee and opening another soda for himself, Mouse sits once again on the chair opposite mine.

Heaving a loud sigh, I preface my story by being straight. "When I came out of the coma, the doctor told me I'd suffered a traumatic brain injury, and that it could affect my head in a myriad of different ways." I huff and dismissively wave my hands. "I ignored his warning, of course. Thought I knew best." Another rush of air leaves my mouth. "To be honest, Mouse, now it's my greatest fear. That what I think has happened over the past couple of days could be all as a result of fucked-up damaged wiring in my head."

"Tell me," he says, simply, his eyes focused as though he's taking every word in.

Taking both a deep breath and the plunge I hope I don't come to regret, I tell Mouse everything. Going to the house, the pictures I took, returning to Bullet's office, meeting Maeve, taking her back to the house, and the things that we saw. It takes me a while to relate, but I leave nothing out. I'm bolstered that he simply looks interested. There's no sign of judgment or scoffing. I even explain how I fell down the stairs, only to come to having apparently fallen exiting my house.

How I ended up in the hospital yet again, and the next morning I revisited Bullet's office to go through the whole thing again. Only, this time, Maeve didn't appear. I'm overly emotional with tears running down my face as I get to the end of my story. I can't even be bothered to care. I sound ridiculous, even to myself, and expect Mouse to start making the arrangements to get me immediately admitted to the nut house.

Instead, he surprises me. Leaning forward, he places his deep tan coloured hand over mine for a second. "Bro, fuck, that's a lot to be dealing with. Give me a moment to unpack it, yeah?"

He sits back, closing his eyes as if meditating.

He's our original tech guru, accustomed to dealing with computers and programming, finding information, and making connections where others might see none. While his tool is a computer, it looks to me like he's currently sifting through everything I've said in his mind, analysing, rearranging, trying out various algorithms to come up with an answer.

I give him space. He doesn't disappoint.

"Maeve Sullivan exists as I said." Suddenly, he sits forward, his hands on his knees. "And get this. You and she were admitted to the hospital at almost the same time. You were in a coma, she is still." He raises his eyes to mine. "What if you met on some spiritual plane? You heard a message she was trying to convey?"

"You're talking nonsense," I retort. "Fuck, Mouse, it doesn't make sense. *Met on a spiritual plane?* You're talking out of your ass."

"*I am?*" Mouse cocks an eyebrow at me. And despite the circumstances, I have to smile.

Although, to my logical mind, it's something I'm inclined to dismiss out of hand. But there are coincidences I can't ignore. Like that Maeve and I were brought to the same medical facility almost simultaneously. How could my imagination have conjured a real, albeit unconscious, person up? Racking my brains, I'm absolutely certain I've never heard of those names before, and Bullet mentioned nothing about them, of that I'm sure.

Mouse suddenly stands. He passes me my crutches. "Come on, I've got an idea."

Bewildered, I get myself upright. "Where we going?"

Jerking his head toward the door, he gives me an explanation. "To the clubhouse, or to my office, to be precise. I like fitting puzzle pieces together, and you've just given me a doozy."

I've just admitted to him I'm fucked in the head, that I've been seeing ghosts. While he might be the one brother in the club who wouldn't straight out laugh at me, or send for a straitjacket, I've no fucking idea why he thinks his computers can help. Unless he has those gadgets you see on paranormal television shows, the ones where they investigate reported hauntings. Narrowing my eyes as I follow after him, I wouldn't actually be surprised if he sent me back to the house with motion detectors or whatever gimmicks they use.

He slows his pace so I can keep up with him, and when he holds the door to the clubhouse open for me, I step/hop inside. It's midafternoon, and there's a prospect half-heartedly cleaning the bar. Tommy, perched on his scooter is fondly looking on as Olivia and Gwen play with their babies in the corner kitted out for kids. They hardly look up as we enter, just giving a brief acknowledgment with a wave of their hands. Ignoring them, Mouse heads straight on, leading me to his office.

Apart from regularly updated equipment, I doubt his domain has changed in the thirty-odd years he's been at the club. It's dark as the blackout blinds are always drawn.

Discreet lighting minimises any glare on the screens, and there, on his desk, is his ever-overflowing ashtray, and next to that, one rolled blunt, and the makings for more.

Pointing me to the chair in front of the desk, he goes to his that's behind it. It comes as no surprise that his first action is to light the blunt, his next to take a deep drag, drawing the smoke in, holding it in his lungs before breathing it out. He offers it to me, but I decline. My head doesn't need to get more fucked than it is. Whatever senses I've got left, I still want around me.

At the click of a few keys, screens flicker to life, and I'm entranced as Mouse gets to work. Watching his hands fly over the keyboard is like seeing a virtuoso pianist in action, his long fingers gliding, frantically tapping, then pausing while his brow scrunches as he reads through results. Rejecting what he finds with a small shake of his head, his lips thin as his hands dance on.

While Mouse is a serious man sitting around the table in church, his face rarely giving away his thoughts, regarding him now, I notice he's far more open. The slight upward curve to his lips and the arching of a brow suggest he might have found something interesting. But it doesn't stop him from clicking the keys and moving on.

Anxious to hear the results of his searching, even though I don't know precisely what he's looking for, I resist the temptation to prompt him for updates, knowing I wouldn't be here if he didn't expect to give me answers.

It seems hours, but it's probably only about ten minutes, before he lifts his fingers from his keyboard, and leans back, linking his hands behind his neck. A shake of his head makes his long hair fly, and he huffs out air to blow a strand off his face.

It's only then that he raises his eyes to me. "Well, I'll be fucked." He turns a screen, angling it so we can both see.

"I started at the source. Emerald and Albert Sullivan." He points to the picture on the screen, and I suck in air as the two people who'd I'd seen getting it on in the bedroom are pictured before me.

What the fuck? It was possible I'd heard Bullet mention Siobhan without taking it in, but there's no way that I'd ever seen the two people in the grainy picture in front of me. Yet, every detail of their faces is just as I remember, complete with the softness in their eyes that shows how much they were in love.

While working, he'd placed the blunt in the ashtray. With a new tremble in my hands, I reach for it and his lighter, picking them both up. I light one end, put my lips to the other, and breathe deeply in.

As Mouse starts summarising their story, I'm grateful. Though it's the same words that are right in front of me, I've lost the ability to focus properly or read. My heart is pounding, and I feel dizzy. Hallucinations are one thing, but how could my brain materialise people who are real?

"They were quite the story back in their day. Albert Sullivan was wealthy, his grandfather having made his fortune in gold here in Arizona and having invested it wisely. Albert's father died during World War I, so he, as the only grandson, inherited everything. He was highly respected and well-known in society. He remained single despite being faced with numerous rich debutantes whose families were courting him. He was in his fifties when he finally fixed his sights on a dancer who definitely came from the wrong side of the tracks. Emerald Dias."

He pauses to shake his head and smirk. "There was obviously

something about her that caught his attention when he saw her on the stage." He stops again to glance at me. "I doubt Emerald was her real Christian name, but I can find no birth certificate. But that was what she used to sign the marriage certificate." He swipes his hair behind his ears again and raises a corner of his mouth. "It was the golden years of the fifties. No one would have blinked an eye if he'd kept her as his mistress. But in nineteen sixty-three, something made him decide to marry her. By then she'd spent ten years performing her arts and had become sought after and popular—among the male crowd." He rolls his eyes. "Her change of status did her no favours in New York. As his wife, it seems she was tolerated, but not welcome in the drawing rooms of the city. He brought her back to his roots, here in Arizona, where his family had generated wealth. He'd renovated the Sullivan House for her, and they took up residence." Mouse clicks a few keys, and a new screen appears. "Seems they had the final joke. They used to throw lavish parties, and people wanting Albert to invest in their businesses either lost the chance or had to come to bumfuck nowhere to tap into his fortune. He used to flaunt Emerald in front of the men who used to leer at her when she was dancing, forcing them to show her respect. I suspect he also enjoyed having captured a woman whom they'd all thirsted over, but who was only his to touch now."

"They really loved each other," I tell him, forgetting that I'm trying hard not to remember how I know, let alone admit it.

Mouse misses nothing. "You saw them?" he asks sharply.

I give a sheepish nod and then shrug. In for a penny... "I saw them at their most intimate."

He chuckles, but softly. "Love can sometimes find itself in the strangest of ways." His eyes glaze slightly, and the upturn to his lips makes me wonder if he's remembering how he met

Mariana. He'd saved her from a bear if I correctly recall the story.

There's a sharp pain in my temple. I place my fingers there, then, in a stupidly plaintive voice, ask him, "But what does this mean? Do the people I saw in my head really exist? What the fuck's going on, Mouse?" My eyes plead with him to help me.

"Vision, not dream or hallucination," he states firmly. "We know you went to the house, you took pictures and showed them to Bullet. But while you were there, the spirits revealed something to you." He rubs at his chin, and his brow furrows. He sweeps his long hair over his shoulder as he asks metaphorically, "But for what purpose? That's what I want to know."

My own brow creases. Could he be right? I'm a twenty-first-century man. It's easier to believe I'm going crazy and that everything I saw had been a figment of my imagination, or nightmares conjured up by the damage from that knock to my skull, than to believe I experienced a prescience of things that were real. My headache seems to worsen with all the conflicting thoughts in my brain.

I return to his question. "You think they were maybe trying to tell me something?" Frowning, I reinforce my question. "Do you really believe that's possible, Mouse?"

Fixing his dark eyes on me, he projects sincerity over the desk that separates us. "If you're asking me whether I believe there's a spirit world that lives alongside us, then my answer has got to be yes. Do I believe in ghosts? Probably, though not the same way as you think, but there are things that we can't explain." He chuckles. "Maybe one day we will. Imagine someone from the nineteenth century being faced with a cell phone, having the ability to contact anyone, anywhere. They'd think that was magic and dismiss it out of hand."

But cell phones are science. I start to argue against him,

then close my mouth. Maybe he's right. In the past, people put volcanic eruptions and earthquakes down to acts of their gods.

Mouse is staring at his screens once again. "Emerald gave birth to two girls."

"Siobhan and Sian." I give him the names immediately.

Raising his chin, he confirms that the facts back up what I was told in my... vision, I suppose, if that's how he wants to describe it. I'm not sure whether to be relieved or dismayed that my imagination hadn't been lying.

"Siobhan was born first, which would make her seventy," he continues. "Sian was born four years later." He keeps clicking, looking from one monitor to the next. "Looks like Siobhan married, but her husband died a while back." Creases appear on his brow. "Albert died in the nineteen-eighties, but Emerald lived on. She passed away in 2010, at the age of seventy. Found a copy of her will. She left everything to Siobhan and nothing to Sian." Again, his fingers fly over the keyboard, then he sighs. "Perhaps this is why. There's a birth registered to Sian in nineteen ninety. She was unmarried." He shakes his head. "Girl gone bad? Mother didn't approve of the relationship? Whatever, that's when Maeve entered the picture."

"She'd almost married," I tell him. "But her fiancé died before they could tie the knot. He was from good folks, but not the stock her grandmother was looking for. Siobhan spun a story that turned Emerald on her younger daughter, though they reconciled before her death. Maeve thought the will had been changed to favour her, but obviously," for some reason I point at his monitor, "it had not."

His sharp eyes narrow. "Maeve told you that?"

Swallowing hard as it seems unbelievable, I simply nod.

He chuckles softly, as if my non-response had been the answer he needed. "As I see it, there's only one thing you can do now. Hound, if I were you, I'd go visit Maeve. I think her grandmother might have been trying to tell you something."

He what? Visit the ghost/spirit, whoever she is, in the hospital? Fuck no. I don't need to struggle to come up with the excuse as to why that's a bad idea. In fact, it's preposterous the more I think about it. "You're suggesting I go visit a woman I've never met before..."

His snort interrupts me. "From the sound of it, you got quite cosy with her."

How he picked up I was attracted to Maeve, I don't know, but it only serves to add yet another complication. I'd feel awkward meeting her. I can't explain that to Mouse without betraying more of myself, so I rely on the most important thing. "What's the fuckin' point if she's unconscious?" Feeling a shiver down my back, I don't voice my next fear. What if the Maeve in the hospital isn't the one I met?

He shrugs. "I don't rightly know, but something tells me this is your path. The coincidence of you both being admitted at the same time can't be dismissed lightly." His shoulders rise up and down. "Maybe she's waiting for you to wake up. Perhaps your presence will bring her around. Or maybe there'll be links to the fucked-up family you found out about." He stands. "Come on. I'll come with you." My expression must speak volumes. Rolling his eyes, he passes my crutches to me. "We've got to go now, or else we'll miss evening visiting time."

CHAPTER TWELVE
MAEVE

I'd apparently come around from a coma, not slowly with a polite regaining of consciousness, but with a gasp, and such a sudden movement from horizontal to vertical that it shocked the fuck out of the nurse who'd come in to monitor the machines in my room. Unprofessionally, she'd screamed.

Even though, to her credit, she'd recovered fast, I was unable to comprehend her words. My mind was assailed by other times, other places, a whole kaleidoscope of colours and images that made no sense. And an overwhelming sensation of a stranger who, for some unknown reason, had become important to me.

Doctors had rushed in, at first concerned that my vitals were triggering warning lights, but as I'd gradually come back to myself, my heart rate slowed, as did their frantic efforts. Finally, when I was breathing at a rate they seemed to accept, they answered the question of why I was lying here, hooked up to machines. Anger caused by the explanation that I was in the hospital as a drunk driver had rammed into my car, and concern when they told me I'd been unconscious for over three weeks, had my blood pressure rising all over again.

I'd been an idiot. I'd no longer had ties to Tucson, so why the hell had I felt driven to come back to visit the remains of my childhood home at this particular time? Damn that sixth sense of mine that seemed to have been pushing me to come. Instead of listening to revived images triggered by dreams, I should have listened to that sane part that told me revisiting my past would just cause me pain and resentment. Though any distress I'd envisaged would have been mental, not physical.

"Steady." One of the doctors places a firm hand on my shoulder. "You really need to stay calm."

I ask the obvious question—what are the extent of my injuries? To which I'm told I suffered a severe concussion and a brain bleed that had eventually stopped. Apparently, I have stitches at my hairline, but I am reassured that my bangs should cover that. I'll be weak due to being laid up for a while, but subject to anything new arising, should now be well on the mend. Well, that's what I interpret from the medical jargon they throw at me.

All I want to know is when I can go home.

The medical staff are cautious due to my abrupt return to reality. I'm told that while my vital signs have already returned closer to normal, I need to have more tests run and remain under observation for perhaps another few days until they can be sure I've suffered no lasting effects. *While the medical expenses build up,* I sardonically think to myself.

That thought makes me query who ran into me and whether they were stopped. Because how else was I going to pay the hospital fees? I'm no millionaire with spare cash lying around.

Those questions are best directed to the police, is their reply, before continuing with their examinations.

After being prodded, poked, blood taken from my arm, and a sample of urine gathered from a container underneath the bed, I'm relieved when finally I'm left alone.

It's then thoughts intrude, a dreamworld weaving around me—sights and sounds entwining, threading, and tangling in ways that can't be sorted out. Recollections as firm as memories of things that can't be possible and must have been dreams and nightmares filling my head while I was unconscious in the morphine-induced nightmare world. *The Sullivan House, both as it had been in its heyday, and ruined by neglect, and then me seeing … ghosts? There was a man, too, such a handsome being only my imagination could have conjured up. Like a common issue with dreams, I can't recall his exact features, but I know there was something about him that attracted me more than it should have. My skin heats as I remember some X-rated scenes that I question how they could have come out of my head. And then, the recall of that odd feature, he was injured himself, hampered by crutches and a broken leg.*

It's true I've never been in a coma before, so I wouldn't know what to expect, but such vivid images are not what I'd have ever thought to bring back to the conscious world with me.

Suddenly, I'm startled by a sound coming from the corridor outside, a peculiar clack repeated in a slow rhythmic manner. For a second, my dreams and reality collide. *It's him. The man who touched me so inappropriately, but so wonderfully, in my family home. Shit. Fuck. Does this mean he was real?* My heart races, causing me to give a concerned glance to the monitors faithfully recording every vital sign. As my sane mind reminds me that I conjured him up in my head, I will my pulse rate to slow. My aim is to get out of here, not to give the nurses a cause for more worry.

But that *clack, clack* is getting louder, the definite sound of something hitting the vinyl floor. Not only that, it reaches a crescendo and then stops right outside my door. There's a perfunctory knock, then it opens into the room.

I suck in air through my teeth, feeling disappointment that it's not my dream man made flesh. Instead, it's my aunt who's approaching, leaning heavily on a cane. It's been fifteen years since I last saw her. Now, pushing seventy-plus, it appears that physically her body is failing. As her eyes, sharp as ever, focus on mine, her face fixed into the familiar scowl, I assume her mind is still active, and her personality not softened from when I first met her as a child.

For a moment, I let the memories take hold of me.

Arriving at this huge house in the middle of nowhere, surrounded by forest, I'd stayed close to my mom's side as she rang the doorbell, totally in awe of a place so grand I expected a butler or at least a maid to answer. Instead, it's a woman who, while stylish and well dressed, is, to me, a fourteen-year-old, older than time.

After the elderly woman stares at my mom for a few awkward moments, my mom introduces herself. "I'm…"

"I may be old, but I've got all my senses. I know who you are," the elderly woman declares. "How could I not recognise the devious features of my own daughter?"

I respond by instinctively moving closer to my mother, unsettled by the hostility directed toward her. Nonetheless, she calmly places a reassuring hand on my arm and, disregarding the severity of her illness, composes herself. "Devious? Is that how you see me?" she replies, her voice measured despite her declining strength. "It is clear you have accepted my sister's account." She shakes her head regretfully. "I thought sufficient water might have flown under the bridge by now."

"You disgraced our family. Fell in with the wrong crowd." Before

Mom can protest, she adds, "So what's brought you crawling back after all these years? You after money?" Her tone is brusque, suspicious.

My mom takes my hand. "Maeve, I'm sorry, sweetheart, there's nothing for us here. It was a waste of time to come. Let's go." She stumbles slightly as she turns, and I give her a supporting hand.

"Wait!" the old woman says sharply. "I demand to know what you want and why you have come?"

Glancing at my mother, I can see she's battling with herself, my young teenage self recognising her pride wants her to just turn her back and leave. But there's more than just her feelings to worry about. There's mine, and what my near future holds.

Taking the time she needs to turn back around, Mom raises her eyes. "Mother, going into care, being fostered, is a life I don't want to impose on my daughter. Maeve will need family around her with what's coming, and you're the only living relative I know. Apart from Siobhan," she adds quickly. "And she'll never lift a finger to keep her niece out of the system."

I hadn't known we were visiting family. As far as I knew, all we had was my dad's, not that I knew him. He died before I was born. Gramps and Granny had given a home to us both, but they'd passed away, leaving us all alone. Mom calls this elderly lady her mother, so I suppose that means she must be my grandmother. It makes me eye the woman in front of me more carefully, but with no love. I've always known that she and my mom were estranged.

"Why do you want to foster your..." she obviously tempers what she was going to say after a glance in my direction. "Child onto me?" It seems it's the first time she's really taken in her countenance. Her eyes narrow as she adds, "You into drugs or something again? Or come back to steal from me?"

Mom breathes in deeply. Her body shudders, and even at my age, I know she doesn't want to admit the truth that she's already carefully and tearfully explained to me. Fighting down my nerves, I address my grandmother directly for the first time. While I might want to spit the awful truth out, I temper my voice, making it quiet and respectful. "Mom's got cancer." Voicing it aloud, I can't help the tears that fill my eyes.

A squeeze of my hand, a proud look down, and Mom takes over from me. "I've got months, Mother. But no more."

For a moment, Mom's words hang heavy in the air. I hold air in my lungs. I doubt there's any happiness to be found inside these doors, and while I'd give everything to have my mom live forever, even at fourteen, I've accepted the truth that, against her will, she'll soon be leaving me all alone. Where would I go?

Even the birds in the trees seem to wait with bated breath as the silence drags on. Then the old woman steps back out of the doorway, raises her hands, and beckons, "Well, you better come in."

Emerald Sullivan. Matriarch of the family, my grandmother, as I came to know, didn't know fuck about the family dynamics. She hadn't known how her elder daughter had poisoned her about her second child, had fed her lies for years, when the truth was that my mother's only crime had been to fall in love with someone Emerald hadn't approved of and had borne a child out of wedlock. The money she was supposed to have stolen? Siobhan had taken it herself, played on her mother's gullibility. The motive? Jealousy.

Growing up, Mom had biased me against my maternal grandmother, bearing resentment herself for Emerald so easily believing Siobhan's lies. I might realise this is my only option to not be alone when Mom can't be with me anymore, but I guard myself against getting too close to the woman who had wronged my mother so much.

While she indeed put a roof over our heads, I was stand-offish over the first few months. Mom was suffering, dying, and Emerald stoically did her duty to her and to me. To this day, I believe it was the crumpled marriage licence she'd found among Mom's effects that made her start to doubt Siobhan was the angel she'd always made herself out to be. The first cracks appeared as the lies became exposed. She began to soften toward Mom and me, and in turn, I began to feel affection for her. After my mom's time came and she was taken from us, hopefully to go to a better place, one with no pain, I'd come to love that old woman, and knew she loved me.

Grandmother, or Gramma, as I came to call her, was my strength, my rock. When she realised the extent of Siobhan's treachery, she said she was going to change her will and leave everything to me. Trouble was, she'd lived a charmed life. Her seventieth birthday came and went, and yet she still felt no urgency to put her affairs to rights. Maybe her brain wasn't as sharp as it was once, or she wasn't as immortal as I think she believed herself to be. But it wasn't her health that failed her. A fall down the stairs that snapped her neck separated me from the only remaining family I had.

Well, not the only person with whom I shared blood, but I'd discounted my aunt as an unpleasant and conniving woman from the first time we met. I wasn't surprised, nor was I particularly upset when Siobhan had stepped in to handle the funeral arrangements, happy to leave it to my aunt. At eighteen, I barely knew enough about living, and nothing at all about the formalities that have to happen when someone dies.

I remember the church was quiet, the mourners numbering only a few. Emerald, a star in her day, had lost touch with or outlived her contemporaries, and since her husband's death, had become a recluse. Siobhan had sat beside me, dry-eyed, as I failed to stop the tears rolling out of mine. I excused her lack of emotion, thinking that age had probably hardened her senses and that she must have been grieving inside.

There was no wake. No point, the few other mourners had

disappeared as soon as her coffin was laid to rest in the ground. Instead, there was a visit to the lawyer's office.

After offering condolences that seemed routine rather than genuine, I waited to hear what provision my grandmother had made for me. I'd lost my mom, and now I'd lost the next most important person to me. I was alone in the world. My aunt and I had never been close, and I doubted she'd want anything to do with me. Even though Gramma had said she'd leave everything to me, I hadn't really thought she'd meant it. But I expected at least some provision, a legacy that perhaps would kick-start and soften this abrupt thrust into adult life.

The will that the lawyer read out was simple. Aunt Siobhan had inherited everything. To me, there was zero. I was left to venture out into the world alone with nothing behind me...

A stick strikes the ground. "I know you're awake, Maeve. The doctors told me."

I hadn't realised I still had my eyes closed. I open them blearily.

"You shouldn't have come back to Tucson. There's nothing for you here."

Fifteen years ago, she'd said something similar. Immediately after the funeral, she'd had no regrets at pushing me out of the house where both my mom and grandmother had taken their last breaths. I had had a few thousand dollars in a savings account my mom had set up for me, and had been paying into it regularly before cancer had taken her down. It was meant to have been my college fund, but I'd had to use it to get out of town and start out on my own.

Grieving and distraught, harbouring the feeling Siobhan had somehow bucked the system as there was no way in hell I'd expected my grandmother to have left her everything, and had given no thought to how I would survive, I took the first Greyhound bus with little care where it was heading. I'd just turned eighteen years old. Even if I had suspicions, how could I prove them? And young as I was, I knew I needed the funds that I had to survive, and not to use them to line lawyers' pockets.

It was my knowledge of my grandmother that drove me to keep my head up and not to give up. She'd had nothing but used the assets she'd been born with to become a celebrated dancer. While I wasn't looking for a man to raise me out of my predicament, I, too, had the urge to do anything I could to keep from going under. While I didn't have the physique or skill that she had, no job was beneath me, and her hard-working ethic was ingrained in my psyche. I waited tables, flipped burgers, and cleaned more hotel rooms than I'd like to count. I paid my own way through college, earning a degree in business. In the end, I'd done alright for myself.

Until that night I'd had the dream.

Everyone sees things while they're asleep, I know that. The mind plays tricks, mixing scenes and people from the long past with those from the present, sometimes so real you doubt yourself when you wake up. But that one had been different. Emerald, adorned in her famous peacock dress she'd always held onto, even though she'd been too old to wear it when I'd met her, had reached out across the decades, warning me, instructing me, to get back to Tucson and save her house. Or rather, something in it. But exactly what, she didn't, or couldn't divulge, as she faded back into the mists of time.

I'd woken with a start, but unlike other dreams which disappeared as soon as I faced the new day, this one stayed with me. My brain kept turning it over and over, unable to forget my grandmother's face or wish to disobey the instruction she'd given me. It played on my mind so much that I was distracted at work.

I had vacation time owing. While acknowledging the

stupidity of it, I booked a week off, believing only a visit to Tucson and the house where I'd lived after my mom had died would get the dream out of my head.

Tap. Tap. Tap tap.

I open my eyes.

"You're back with me," Siobhan states. "Stay with me, girl." I'm a woman, thirty-three years old. Not long returned to the waking world, I don't have the energy to correct her. But when she continues, in that annoying nasally tone of hers, "Try to concentrate." I snap.

"I was badly injured in a car accident, and have only just come out of a coma. Forgive me if I can't pay you the attention you want. Best you spit out what you want to say before I decide sleep's more important."

She bristles. I doubt anyone's ever called her out on her behaviour. "Mind your manners," she retorts, prodding at her coiffured hair that's got so much spray on it, it doesn't move. "I want to know why you've come back to Tucson. There's nothing for you here." She pauses a beat, but I don't answer. How can I? How could I admit a dream brought me here? As to my desire to visit the house, it belongs to her, and I've no right to step one foot in it. Then she surprises me. "You had it right. Taking what money you had and getting out of here. That house is nothing but trouble. I couldn't afford to live in it. No one wants to buy it. Now it's structurally unsound, so my only option is probably to demolish it. Not that the land's worth anything much."

"When?" I ask sharply, her words bringing sudden clarity to my mind.

"As soon as possible."

"I want to visit before it's knocked down." I can't admit I'm driven to search for whatever my dream tells me is hidden. And there are those visions, dreams, and prescience that are nagging in the back of my mind, telling me in my coma that somehow I already visited the house. That can't be true, but it cements my desire.

"Impossible. The place is condemned. You'd risk your life if you stepped inside."

CHAPTER THIRTEEN
HOUND

Mouse holds me back when we approach the hospital room he's discovered Maeve is in, as we hear voices from within. He places a finger to his lips.

"Impossible. The place is condemned. You'd risk your life if you stepped inside." The speaker's voice sounds elderly, both sharp and unpleasant. After a pause, she continues, "This whole trip was a waste of time. Look what happened to you. You should have left well alone and stayed where you came from."

"I want to see the house, Siobhan," a decidedly younger voice asks, and one, *fuck it,* that sounds familiar. My heart pounds. Crazy or clairvoyant? What the hell am I supposed to think? I brush those thoughts aside and concentrate on eavesdropping.

"Why now? You've had fifteen years to visit the place, yet you never came home."

"Why have you held onto it all this time?" she counters. "Why let it fall to ruin, so the only option is to knock it down?"

"You think I haven't tried to get rid of it before now?" the old woman hisses. "It's the only thing of any value my mama left to me, but instead of setting me up for life, it's been a millstone around my neck. I've tried to sell it, but there have been no buyers. And all the real estate agents have refused to have it on their books for one reason or another." Her voice is getting angrier. "I even tried to burn it down, but the damn fire wouldn't take."

I catch Mouse's eye and give him a meaningful nod to convey I'd seen the evidence of attempted arson with my own eyes.

"The only option I have is to raze that hateful place to the ground and try to make whatever bank I can on the land."

"I still want to see it before you pull it down," Maeve states firmly.

"Well, you can't. I forbid it. I'm going to the developers' office now and insist that they start the demolition straight away."

"Siobhan, Aunt, please. I won't even go inside. Just let me see it for old time's sake. I've got so many memories there."

"You've had those memories for fifteen years, yet you've never come back before. I don't understand your sudden interest now. I won't wait. That house is coming down."

Not if I've got anything to do with it. A word in Bullet's ear will mean the work will go to the back of the queue. Whatever reason Maeve has for wanting to see inside, I won't let her lose the chance. The old woman's voice is grating on me. My immediate dislike for her puts me on her niece's side.

"Siobhan…"

"I wish you well."

With that blatantly insincere comment, there's the sound of wood hitting the floor. Mouse and I step back and take poses as if we've just closed the door to the next room.

An elderly, well-dressed woman with her nose in the air brushes past us without looking us in the eye. A waft of rose water floats in the air as she turns the corner and disappears out of sight.

Stepping through the door of the hospital room, the words spill out of my mouth. "If you want to see the Sullivan House, you can. It's rickety, but if you're careful, it's not too dangerous…" My words trail off as I catch sight of the woman in the bed. I heard her speak, but seeing her in the flesh? My voice trembles. "Maeve?" My head starts to spin as a veritable ghost meets my eyes. I feel Mouse's hand on my arm, keeping me upright.

"Who the hell are… *you?*"

Mouse looks from me to her, then steps forward and takes charge. "Maeve, I'm Mouse," he tells her. "Your name is Irish?"

Politeness wins over the perplexed expression on her face. "Yes," she replies to him. Then her eyes narrow on me, her head cocked to one side. Her brow is furrowed as she takes me in from head to toe, and she swallows with an audible gulp. I'm thinking she's recognised me, but then she shakes her head as if to clear it and asks, "Do I know you? There's something about you that's familiar." There's a quaver in her voice.

What the hell? Her question makes my palms sweat. She's been in the hospital ever since I was injured. "We've never met," I refute sharply. That's the truth. Definitely not in the flesh.

Mouse squeezes his fingers on my arm that he still holds, as he murmurs softly, "You haven't met in this world."

Instead of scoffing at his enigmatic statement, Maeve looks bewildered. After examining him carefully, she asks, "You're Native American?"

"Half-Navajo," he confirms.

Pressing a button, she raises the top of the bed. Examining

her for a moment, I realise how different she looks from the version of her I met in my dreams. Her face is pale and wan, her hair not so glossy and sleek. *She's only just out of a coma,* I remind myself. I suspect I looked no better when I first awoke. A wave of sympathy goes through me. *We shouldn't be here bothering her.* But then, how am I to get the answers to what's wrong in my head? Brain damage can't summon up someone who's real, can it?

"I don't understand why you're here." Her eyes flit to Mouse, but as they focus on me, I see the tinge of concern.

Uninvited, Mouse pulls up a chair by the bed. "You might think it bizarre that two strangers have come to visit you, but we mean you no harm. Hound," he points to me, "has visited the Sullivan House."

His explanation does nothing to reassure her. She turns paler if that's possible and breathes in a sharp breath. "You were in the house."

It's a statement, not a question. *Am I not mad? Was she really there too?* There's something about her reaction that makes me believe there's something she's not saying.

Mouse continues gently, "Your aunt instructed our club's construction company to make an assessment of the Sullivan House. She might try to order us to demolish it, but we make up our own minds about our jobs. We overheard her talking to you." He looks completely unashamed at his admission. "We figured out that a delay, at least, would be beneficial to you."

Her focus returns to him. "Why would you do that? You don't know me."

"I know you've got connections to the place. Do you want to tell us why it's so important that you go back to it?"

Her eyes still fixed on him, her words come out as if in a trance. "I lived there. I left here when Emerald, my grand-mother, died fifteen years back. I couldn't believe she'd left me nothing, but I couldn't fight my aunt. I felt betrayed and never, ever, wanted to return to Tucson. It was bittersweet. I had good memories of living with my grandmother, but those were overpowered by the resentment I'd felt. I put it behind me and moved on with my life. Until I started having dreams. Something was calling me back." Her head suddenly shakes. She breaks eye contact, and raises her fingers to her forehead. "I'm sorry, I've no idea why I spilled all that."

Mouse leans toward her and pulls her hand away from her eyes. Once he's again gained her attention, he jerks his head in my direction. "Hound's had a vision that he met you in that house."

As she stiffens, Mouse pulls back, putting distance between them. Maeve moves her head side to side once more. She opens her mouth, then presses her lips together. Lips I so fondly remember touching mine. Her eyes close briefly, then she reopens them. She takes a deep breath, swallows, but if she was going to say something, the words don't come out.

Was she there in her dreams, or were they mine? She looks so damn familiar. She's definitely the woman I saw in my head. Could the figment of my brain injury really be lying in front of me? And I didn't just see her, *I'd fingered her sexually for fuck's sake. Felt her orgasm beneath my fingers.* Noticing her face has gone from pale to bearing two large patches of red on both cheeks, I wonder if she's having the same recollection. Nah, I'm the one suffering hallucinations.

"You couldn't have seen me," she dismisses, with a nervous and forced laugh. "I've been unconscious in this bed for weeks." But something about the way she says it leaves me with that doubt. As does the fact that she doesn't question my sanity. "Tell me, if you went there, is it as bad as my aunt said? Was it dangerous to visit?"

As an answer, I take out my phone, click on photos, and

summon up the recent images. *Thank fuck.* The pictures appear that I'd taken of the Sullivan House. I've proof that I've been there, and that at least some of the last couple of days weren't all imaginings conjured up in my head.

Approaching her, I offer my phone. "I went to the house…" *a day ago? A week?* I decide to leave the timescale out of it. "This is what it looks like now. Is this what you saw?"

She takes the phone from me. I position myself beside her head so I can watch her reaction to the photos. The first few she skims through after giving me a curious look, and I wryly indicate the crutches I'm using. She views the ones approaching the house more slowly, sucking in a breath, halting on the image of the front porch. For a second, I see her eyes close and she breathes in deeply.

"I never thought I'd come back," she murmurs. "I knew my mom was dying when she took me to meet Emerald. At first, I was scared by the reception we received, but it soon emerged that lies had been told, and that Siobhan was behind it. It was in that house that Mom took her last breath. Gramma had arranged for hospice care there. My grandmother regretted the years she'd lost having banished my mother, and tried to make up for it by caring for me. She was this amazing, larger-than-life person. I doubt there was anyone else in the world who could have comforted me and seen me through my grief at losing my only parent. This," she taps the front porch showing in the photo, "represents some of the worst, and some of the best times of my life."

She waits for no comment, not indicating that she needs one. She moves on to the next picture, and then the ones that follow. Some make her mouth quirk in a private smile as if remembering words spoken or deeds done in that location.

As she nears the one where, in my dream version of the

visit to Bullet's office, she had identified her grandmother in the frame, I hold my breath, hoping she'll see nothing and move on. But she gasps. With a shaking hand, she reaches out a trembling finger. "That's her. That's my grandmother. She's still in the house."

"It's a figment of the light," I repeat Bullet's words to her. "There's no one there."

She turns, looks at me, and then places her hand on my arm, grasping it far stronger than a woman just woken from a coma should be able to do. "Can you swear to me you were alone in that house?"

I try to wrench my hand away, but she holds onto it firmly. I tug once more, only serving to make her dig her fingernails into my skin. Before she can draw blood, something breaks inside me, and I vomit out what I believe is the truth.

"Fuck it, Maeve. I've got to tell you upfront, I had an accident about the same time as you. Like you, I ended up in a coma, but came out of it sooner. I'm suffering from a traumatic brain injury. I see things, suffer hallucinations." I take a breath but carry on before she can comment. "These visions are so fuckin' real." I pause to huff a strangled laugh. "In my head, I'm convinced I showed all these pictures to Bullet, who's, well, for this purpose, my boss. While I was in his office, Maeve, you came to meet with him, looked through the photos, and stopped on the very same one." Maeve's sharp inhale doesn't stop me from continuing to spew out all the rubbish in my head as I tell her how "dream Maeve" insisted she be given access to the house. Despite my reservations, I had agreed and taken her back. "I can clearly remember us exploring the house together. And yeah, if you want to know the worst of my fucked-up brain, I believed I saw Emerald as she was when she was younger, along with Bertie, her husband." I stop talking, not wanting to mention the kiss or the further intimacies either they, or we got up to.

Maeve holds my gaze for a moment, then her head falls back on the pillow, her eyes rolling back until nothing is showing but white. The machines start beeping, and a nurse rushes in, her face contorted in concern.

"Get out of here," the nurse states, lowering the head of the bed and pushing a big red button on the wall.

Mouse starts toward the door, but I can't move. I'm frozen to the spot. But as more medical staff rush in, I'm manoeuvred out into the hallway, and the door closes, locking us out.

"What the fuck have I done?" I roar.

Mouse moves fast, his hand gripping my shoulder. "She's had a bad accident," he says fast. "I doubt if anything you said caused her to relapse. She's probably got a ticking time bomb in her head."

"Like me," I say self-deprecatingly.

"For fuck's sake, Hound. You're still on the mend."

I look at him incredulously. "You hearing yourself, Brother? You heard the shit I spouted in there. What sane person could listen to that?"

"Me," he says fiercely. "I've seen things, heard things, experienced shit that you'd mock at."

I grab hold of his arms. "But I'm not you," I cry out. "I can't believe anything I'm seeing is real. I'm going out of my fuckin' mind. Am I even here?" I jerk my head toward the closed door beside us. "And if I am, I might have killed her."

As I speak, said door opens, and the medical staff start coming out. A nurse pauses beside us. "Family?" she asks.

"Yes," Mouse says.

"No," I respond at the same time.

She shakes her head and defers to my companion. "It was a blip. She'll be fine."

"Let's get out of here." I accompany my words with action, hurrying down the corridor to get out of this place.

"Wait up," Mouse entreats. "Maeve might want to talk to you again."

I spin around. "The shit in my fucked-up brain almost killed her! I'm not going near her again."

CHAPTER FOURTEEN
MAEVE

The house is brightly lit, the light from the hall chandelier reflecting off the walls. Candles are alight in their holders, sending warmth flickering through the main room which sports the tallest Christmas tree I've ever seen, adorned with coloured lights, baubles and tinsel, and with an angel placed on top. Even as a teenager, my attention was caught, captivated by the magic of the season.

My nose twitches as aromas reach me from the kitchen, pulling me that way. Once this house had servants, a butler, maids and a cook. Nowadays, it's just my grandmother and my mom. The only parent I've ever known who I'll lose only too soon.

Chemo is taking it out of my mother. She barely resembles the woman who nurtured me during my childhood. Her skin is almost translucent, and her form nigh on skeletal. She'd known she'd lost the battle with cancer before we had stepped foot in this house. I knew only too well how damn hard it was for her to admit she'd been beaten by the disease. And how, along with the cancer cells, she was riddled with guilt about what would happen to me, while all I hoped for was a miracle.

Rather than bursting in through the kitchen door, I stand back as I hear the word, *hospice,* and start listening intently.

"You're my daughter," I hear my grandmother say. "My blood and your father's run through your veins. I'm not letting you go and die among strangers. I've money. I'll pay to have someone provide medical attention to you here in this house."

"Momma, you can't afford it." My mom's voice, far weaker than it should be, scolds her. "You're rattling around in this place with no one to clean or look after you. I'd rather you kept what you have for yourself."

A peal of laughter follows. "Sian, my love, you think because I have no one waiting on me that I'm poor? Good God, woman, but after you caused so much trouble..." she pauses, then adds in a harsher tone, "or I was led to believe that you had, I was fed up with the servants gossiping. I got rid of them all. The garden can go to hell as far as I'm concerned, and I'm quite happy to keep the place tidy and cook for myself. What else is an old woman to do?" Her voice softens. "I didn't come from riches. I knew hard work. Knew what it was like to have callouses on my hands from working for rich folk. I was lucky that I became Emerald and hit pay dirt when I caught Bertie's eye. And what a catch he was." Her tone becomes whimsical as she confides, "I know some said I led him on and took advantage of him, but they were all wrong. I loved him with all my heart. He was such a wonderful man. Since he died, I've just been waiting to join him, but life can be cruel and keeps dragging on." Her voice catches. "It's not fair that I'm still here and he's gone. Except..." a pause, and I can't see her, but I can imagine her hugging my mom. "Perhaps my purpose was to take care of you, Sian, after the injustice I did to you."

"Momma..."

"No, don't you feel sorry for me, Sian. While most of my good times were in my past, you and that lovely daughter of yours have brightened my world since you darkened my doorstep. And when you're gone, I promise I'll look after Maeve." She pauses to chuckle softly. "And not just because you gave her a good Irish name."

Mom's chuckle makes me smile. I've heard too little of that lately.

For a moment, there's a clattering of pans, the sounds of chopping, and I'm just about to reveal myself, when Emerald speaks again. "Sian, I'm sorry about what happened. I still can't believe Siobhan fooled me with her lies."

"I'm sorry too," Mom replies. "But it's the truth. Siobhan accused me of the things she herself was doing."

"You did get pregnant by that man…"

"He was a good man. Our only crime was pre-empting things by having sex before we married, but I had a ring on my finger and the wedding arranged. Did you wait until your nuptials before you knew Dad in an intimate way?"

There's a pause, then Gramma chuckles. "Actually, I did. I'd had two choices when dancing—give it away to anyone and everyone, hoping for a few trinkets to come my way, or save it for someone special."

There's a pause, then Mom answers, "I know Siobhan intimated I was playing around, but Dave was my first, my only. Sure, we should have waited for the wedding bells to ring, but I wouldn't have had it any other way. It was a twist of fate that I fell pregnant when I lost my virginity. Had we waited, Maeve would never have been born. She's my memory of the one man who I loved and lost."

"You could have come home and told me…"

"But you'd thought I'd stolen five thousand dollars!" Mom sounds exasperated. "You thought I'd taken the money to give to a man who'd make nothing of himself except use it to buy drugs. Sure, he and his family weren't rich, but they were hard-working and made enough to get by. Dave was a proud man. He'd have taken no handouts and definitely not stolen cash."

I hear the smacking of hands and can picture Grammy brushing flour off her skin. There's quiet, then, she says, "Siobhan told me he got you pregnant and then left you alone. I presumed he'd run through the money by then."

Mom sighs. "Kind of the truth, but twisted. Dave couldn't help dying." Her voice breaks. "I just wish I'd known him longer, and he'd had the chance to meet Maeve. And...you." She says the last hesitantly.

"Oh, honey. Now I know the truth, I do too. I was a blind, stupid woman who didn't see through the lies. When Siobhan came here wearing her fancy dresses, I just thought her husband was being generous, and not that she'd taken the money herself."

"Mom..."

There's rustling. I can't see, but I'm imagining them in each other's arms. After a couple of minutes of silence, I'm about to put in an appearance when Gramma speaks again.

"I asked Siobhan to look for you, but she came back with a story I shouldn't have accepted. She said you'd shacked up with druggies and left the state, having gotten the cops after you for robbing stores. I should have suspected Siobhan was up to something. She was jealous of you from the time you were born. I tried to treat both of you girls equally, but you were so pretty, dainty, and took after me, while Siobhan inherited your dad's looks. Pretty enough in her own way, but nothing to match the grace of my youngest daughter. You were a dancer, Siobhan had two left feet. I hate admitting it, but maybe I'd had a preference back then and let it be known. Until you started, or apparently began, acting up. The evidence brought to me by Siobhan."

"It was Siobhan who frequented the parties, did drugs and shoplifted. I was never capable of anything like that. But you didn't believe me, so when I met Dave, I had my opportunity to move on." Mom pauses, then adds, "And when you discovered the money missing, I knew you'd never believe I was innocent if I came back. I knew how plausible Siobhan could be."

"I hate to admit it, but time's proven your version is right." I hear a deep sigh. "Siobhan's made her bed and must lie in it. Don't worry about Maeve, I'll look after her when..."

"When I'm gone."

"Then Maeve will inherit everything I have. This house, and whatever money is left.".

My mom doesn't comment. When the only sounds are of two women cooking again, I come around the doorway and enter the room, my mouth watering at the delights they've already made, my stomach grumbling in anticipation. Neither of them has noticed me, and with the sudden realisation that this will be the last Christmas I spend with my mother unless a miracle happens, I approach and place my arms around her. Yet, it's not her comforting body I feel, but thin air, my hands only meeting themselves.

Now the odours reaching my nose are those of decay and mould. The light has gone. Only the glimmer of the fading sun lights the room, casting long shadows. There's no food, and no one here except me.

My heart rate increases. I'm aware of every little sound. There are creaks and groans of an old house settling, but no cheery voices like I heard before. I know I'm in the Sullivan House, but it's not as I know it. Time has passed. Feelings of loss sweep over me as I realise both my mom and grandmother have long gone. I'm not a teenager anymore. I'm a grown woman.

But how did I get here? If this is a dream, I want to wake up. When pinching myself doesn't work, I feel panic rising. This house, that seemed so welcoming and familiar just moments ago, has transformed into something foreboding and dark. Trickles of fear like icy water run down my spine, not helped when a splattering of white plaster falls like confetti from the ceiling above.

I turn to move to the door through which I entered, but I feel like I'm walking through molasses, my legs like lead, anchored to the ground. I struggle to take one step, but the exit seems no closer. Blood's pounding through my veins, and I just want to escape.

Another hard-earned step, but the way ahead seems elongated.

"Maeve?"

It's the voice of the man who was in my hospital room. The man I was sure I'd met before. The location? In my dreams, which is absurd.

"I'm here, Maeve. Just follow my voice."

My ears lock onto the direction of the sound, and my legs feel lighter as I gain ground.

"That's it, come closer. You're almost here. Reach for my hand."

Taking another step, I stretch out my fingers, dreading that the sounds of hope are going to prove an illusion once again. But a warm hand clutches mine, pulling me forward and into the light.

"She's back," someone announces.

Now my ears hear the beeping of hospital monitors, and my eyes open to see a smiling nurse staring into my eyes. "No need to worry," her soft voice reassures me. "Your heart rate just became erratic for a moment, your blood pressure dropped, and you passed out."

I swallow once, then again, trying to moisten my mouth, then I ask in a husky voice, "How long was I unconscious?"

"Only a minute," the nurse replies.

Though I try to keep my eyes locked on hers, I feel the blackness threatening once more, and there's nothing I can do to stop it sweeping over me.

CHAPTER FIFTEEN
MOUSE

Reluctantly, I drive Hound back to the compound. It may be wrong, but I'm questioning leaving Maeve alone when there's something inside of me that says we should have stayed there to support her. I know Hound's feeling guilty, blaming himself for telling too much to her, so much that it seemed to cause her heart to stop.

In his mind, he thinks he almost killed her. It's obvious, he's drifted off to sleep and is murmuring words that are hard to make out, but enough so I know he's dreaming about her, shifting restlessly and repeating something like, *take my hand, Maeve, I'm here.*

Brought up as an all-American boy, I lived in Tucson until I was in my teens and my dad died. My mom was a proud Navajo, but she'd been swept off her feet by a white man. Taken away from the reservation, she'd brought me up with no knowledge of her side of the family. I knew nothing of the conflict within her, only knowing she'd embraced the modern American life, until my dad left us. I went from being a nerd kid who liked nothing more than playing computer games to being uprooted and living on a reservation with the Navajo side of my family, with barely any electricity and no Wi-Fi in sight.

I didn't fit in. At first, I rebelled, refused to accept my changed life, until I began to learn I was neither white man nor Native, but something in between. Gradually, my new world began to make sense, and I began to marry both halves. Things that Tse, the kid who was brought up in Tucson, would scoff and laugh at started to become second nature to the Tse living with my Navajo relatives. Skinwalkers, a concept I'd first scoffed at, became a reality to me, along with other things we can't name or even see, but which walk among us. It made more sense to me than the Anglo's religion.

Unlike white folks, the Navajo encourage visions and place meaning on dreams.

If any other of my Satan's Devils brothers had heard what Hound had to say, then they'd certainly believe he was simply suffering the effects of his traumatic brain injury. With me, though, the jury's still out.

I ponder puzzle pieces, loving nothing more than finding snippets of information, and then rearranging them again and again until they form a complete picture. Combine that with my beliefs that there's more to the world than we could ever imagine, and I didn't immediately dismiss Hound's apparent ravings out of hand.

It was when I researched and discovered the truth behind the things he couldn't possibly have known that I knew I was needed to help and support him.

The module in my truck triggers the gate to automatically open as we approach. In the past, we used to have the prospects man it. Now they do so, but from comfortable surroundings, observing a screen. As normal for anything with four wheels, I pull up behind the shop.

Hound jerks awake as the vehicle stops. Rubbing his eyes, he looks at me apologetically. "Hell, I'm sorry, didn't mean to drop off."

"You're exhausted. No one can blame you." Glancing at him, concerned, wondering whether I should have driven further up the track, I ask, "You okay to walk from here, Brother?"

"Of course, I fuckin' am." As if to prove it, Hound doesn't wait for me to open his door and help him. He gets out by himself and, balancing on his good leg, manages to get his crutches from the rear seat. It means I end up a pace behind him as he swings and hops his way up the slope.

When it looks like he intends to bypass the clubhouse, I catch up. "Come in, Brother. Get a drink. You don't want to be alone."

He pauses, wavers for a moment, takes a longing look up the rest of the incline that leads to his house, then there's that slow dip and rise of his head that I'm waiting for. Holding the clubroom door open for him, I'm relieved he's stopping by. Being alone and lost in his head isn't helpful right now.

Hound thinks it's his brain playing tricks on him. I think it's something else. Rather than something to be feared, it could be a portal has opened to him. Or, it was always there, and his damaged synapses have finally let him see it.

"Mouse!" Drummer, standing by the bar, raises his hand and beckons me over. I steer my companion that way. He raises his chin as I draw close. "Was wondering where you got to, Mouse. Coke." The last, accompanied by a head jerk, is to the prospect behind the bar. Then, to the man accompanying me, "Beer, Hound?" As Hound nods, the prospect has a bottle opened and ready without being asked.

Me with my soda, Hound, now perched on the barstool with his beer, and Drummer sipping sedately at his notorious top-shelf scotch, we drink in comfortable silence for a moment.

"Brothers," comes a deep voice.

I don't need to turn to identify the speaker. It's Peg. As he comes alongside, I see Blade has entered with him.

When Drummer, Peg, Wraith and Blade had stepped down from their officer roles, I'd have been willing to go with them, but while Wizard, our prez, my brother-in-law's computer skills now exceed mine, I was asked to stay on. Not that I've ever been an official officer, but I've an important tech role on the team. Likewise, Dollar, our treasurer, wasn't allowed to retire, as there was no one better to take his role.

But it's a bit like old times now, us F.O.G.s, as the youngsters call us, sticking together and, while the young'uns heal, take back the direction of the club.

"Hey, Wraith," Drummer calls out. "Wondered if you were going to join the party."

"Not much of a fuckin' party," Wraith comments as he draws close, accepting the beer the prospect offers. He glances at me, Peg, Drummer, and then Blade. "Thought we'd at least have some fun while the young 'uns were getting themselves together. This place has been quiet as the grave."

Blade flexes his arthritic hands, grimacing as he does so. "Be careful what you wish for, *VP.*" His mouth quirks. Like the rest of them, Wraith's only stepping back into this role temporarily.

Hound murmurs something into his beer.

"What was that, Bro?" Peg asks.

"I said you can have your old job back permanently. I won't be riding as sergeant-at-arms again." As mouths fall open around him, he pauses, then adds, "If I ride at all."

"Snap out of it, man," Drummer barks. "Sure, you've got

enough metal in your leg to set off a detector at twenty feet, but you'll heal and will be riding again."

Peg's face is going red. "You've got a broken leg, Hound. Bad as it might be, at least you've got two working lower limbs. You really want to go there when it's me you're talking to?"

Uh uh. Peg's been living and riding with a prosthetic leg for years. Never stopped him from being the best damn sergeant-at-arms in the club.

As Hound raises his hand to his head, I go to preempt whatever he's going to say with a warning. Moving in close, I hiss at him, "Don't say a fuckin' word." But I know he's not going to heed me. "Hound," I growl again.

Drummer's steely eyes harden as he looks from me to Hound. "What's going on?"

But at the precise moment Hound opens his mouth to probably lay the extent of what he perceives to be his brain injury in front of them, instead of speaking, his eyes glaze over, his jaw slackens, and as if in slow motion, he slips to the floor. If it wasn't for Drummer's quick thinking, he'd have fallen flat on his face. As it is, our temporary prez gently lets him down to the ground.

"Call 911," Peg barks to the prospect.

"No!" I say sharply.

"No? What the fuck do you mean?" His steely eyes bore into me as he repeats his request. "Call for a bus, Prospect."

"Put the damn phone down," I yell at Razza. "Drummer, there are things you don't know."

"I fuckin' know I've got an injured man lying unconscious on the floor," he growls. As he starts to gesture to Razza again, I grab hold of his hand.

He swings me around and has my back against the bar. "You want him to die?"

"Fuck no I don't want that. But there's more to this, Drummer."

"You better start fuckin' talking, Mouse." He holds onto the side of my cut and shakes me.

I speak fast. "Hound thinks he's suffering from a TBI, but that's not all that's going on, Prez." At his raised brow, I continue, "Bullet sent him to visit the Sullivan House, an abandoned mansion in the foot of the hills. He was fine until he went there, and a fuckin' mess since he came back. There's something wrong there, Drummer."

He straightens, sending a look to Peg, then to Wraith and Blade. "What are they doing at that fuckin' house? Making meth?"

Taking a breath to centre myself, I try to find the words that could possibly help me explain the situation to my brothers in the club. They're one hundred percent Anglo, brought up differently from me, without the Native blood running in their veins. Had I not been taken to the reservation when I was a teen, I'd have probably been viewing the situation exactly the same as them.

"There are things outside of our experience," I start, choosing my words carefully. "Some things aren't black and white, and not all time follows a continuum."

"Speak fuckin' English, Bro," Blade admonishes. I don't miss the knife that's appeared in his right hand. Even though his fingers are bent, he's still managing to juggle it expertly. "All I can see is that we've got a man down and you don't want to raise a finger to help him."

"Hound thinks he's been hallucinating. I think it's more than that." I take a deep breath, hoping they remember my history, and the years they've ridden with me, and don't immediately summon the men in white coats with strait jackets to take me away. "I think he's seen spirits."

"Whisky? Brandy?" Peg quips.

Drummer waves his hand at him. "You serious, Mouse?"

Before I can answer, Hound starts moving at our feet, not regaining consciousness, but moving in an agitated way. His hands come up as if to battle an enemy, and out of his mouth comes a stricken plea, "Maeve, don't go in there. Keep back!"

With the exception of Peg, who has only one working leg, he's not so agile, the rest of us fall to our knees with a variety of creaks that show our age.

"Hound," I admonish, giving him a shake. "Hound. What the fuck's happening?"

I almost fall back on my heels as he opens his eyes, catches mine, his wide with distress as he says clearly, "Maeve's at the house. She needs help."

"Maeve?" Drummer snaps.

Quickly, I fill him in while at the same time helping Hound to his feet as he's struggling to get up on his own. "Maeve's a woman who has a connection to that fuckin' house, and she was in a coma at the exact same time as him." Passing Hound his crutches, I try to get Drummer on side. "I know you'll find this hard to believe, but Maeve and Hound met in their dreams, while they were unconscious." Drummer's eyes go to the heavens, Blade barks a laugh, and Peg snorts. Wraith is just watching me warily. "Look, I know this sounds crazy, but if Hound thinks Maeve's at the house and that she's in danger, well, that's enough for me." Hound's frantically trying to get loose from my hold, so to him I say, "I got you, Brother. I'm coming with you."

"He needs a hospital." Wraith steps in front of us, barring our way.

"He needs to see this through," I contradict, my arm around Hound, feeling how tense and wound up he is.

Drummer's eyes glare into me. "You really taking him to the Sullivan House?"

Hound speaks for himself, clearly having regained some strength. "If he doesn't, I'll drive myself. Ain't no one stopping me. I've got to get to Maeve."

His challenge stands for nothing. He's a one-legged man, helpless if anyone takes his crutches away.

"Oh fuck it," Blade states, grinning widely. "We've got a sergeant-at-arms who thinks he's seeing things, and believing he has to go rescue a damsel in distress." He waves his hand around at the decorations in the clubhouse, put there for the kids who had a party earlier. "It's fuckin' Halloween. I'm up for a ghost hunt. I'm going with Mouse."

Wraith's still blocking our route. I hesitate before ploughing through him and pushing him out of our way, especially when I see him give a querying glance toward Drummer.

Drummer sighs loudly, places his whisky glass down on the bar with a thump, then shakes his head. "So either Wizard's got a sergeant-at-arms with a traumatic brain injury that will end his ride with the Devils, or he's really been seeing ghosts." He shakes his head. "Can't believe I'm fuckin' saying this, but I'm coming with you. Got to sort this out one way or another."

"Not leaving me out," Peg states.

"Life's been too fuckin' boring," Blade says. "Lead the way."

Wraith's eyes gleam. "Kids have too much fun on Halloween. Think it's time us old men got in on that." He flexes his gnarly hands. "Ghost hunting? Bring it the fuck on."

CHAPTER SIXTEEN
HOUND

Mouse gets me seated in one of the club's SUVs while the revving of motorcycle engines fills the air. Right now, I'd donate a kidney if it meant I could be riding a two-wheeler alongside my brothers. Even if my leg was good, with my damaged brain, I doubt that's something I'll ever be able to do again. I wouldn't be surprised if I lose my licence and can't even drive a cage. Who wants someone who blacks out at the drop of a hat controlling any type of vehicle?

And now I've got the whole club—or a significant part of it—following me on a fool's errand. They're only coming along as I'd had yet another vision, for fuck's sake. This one telling me Maeve is in danger, yet the rational part of me screams it's all in my fucked-up head. There's no way I can know anything about her, let alone her whereabouts and needs. Realistically, why should she even be at the Sullivan House? Last I knew, her physical body was still in the hospital, hooked up to machines.

Yet, somehow, Mouse has convinced everyone to come along for the show—the one where they all end up knowing what a freak I've become. As we leave the compound, I convince myself that we're just going to see a derelict house, unoccupied by anything living or otherwise. My hands form fists as I realise tonight might be the time I'm asked to give back my patch. Or, at least temporarily surrender it while the psychiatrists figure out where my head's at, and whether the damage is permanent.

The sun's setting below the horizon, and darkness falls as we head toward Tucson, turning off before we get into the city to head for the Sullivan House set in the foothills. As the roar of the motorcycles following reaches me, I wonder how the hell I'll cope when my brothers discover what a fuckup I am.

For a moment, I blame Mouse. It's he who believes in spirits and the supernatural, not me. If it wasn't for him, I'd put everything down to hallucinations. Even though Wizard is still confined to the hospital with both legs in traction, I now think I've come off the worst. Broken bones will mend, but a damaged brain? Nah, ain't no cure for that. And Mouse is just making things worse by trying to translate the visions in my fucked-up brain and attempting to ground them in reality.

I take my role as sergeant-at-arms, the protector of the club, seriously. I don't want Peg to regain that position permanently. But I have to accept that I'm no longer the man who should be trusted with that officer role in the club. If I can't have faith in myself, no one else should want to follow me.

While part of me wants to insist Mouse stop this charade and turn the car around to head back to the clubhouse, another part thinks this is exactly what I deserve. We'll arrive at the Sullivan House, find it's just another decaying monstrosity of times gone by, no ghosts, no Maeve. And then I won't have to pretend anymore.

It's that side that wins out. I stay silent on the drive,

promising myself that if everything goes to shit, there's always a bullet in my gun that can end my suffering.

When Mouse turns into the gate that I'd left open on my previous visit, and proceeds up the drive, the flash of lightning doesn't even surprise me, though I don't expect that my brothers will share the apprehension of impending doom. At least I can relax in the knowledge that my brain injury affects only me, and that they won't experience anything but an abandoned and neglected empty house. Though they may have a word to say about the track that certainly isn't suitable for bikes.

We pull up, get out of the car, and have to wait for a few minutes for the bikes to come to a stop behind us. From their grimaces and the way Blade checks his ride, they'd found the track a challenge.

The sudden silence once all engines are cut off is oppressive. Until there's the sound of another engine coming up the driveway.

All turning at once, we look to see who the fuck has come out on this stormy night to visit the Sullivan House.

When the chauffeured car stops, Mouse and I both recognise the woman stepping out.

It's Mouse who hisses the warning. "That's Siobhan Sullivan. She owns this house."

"And Maeve is?"

Suspecting Drummer's asking for clarification on the relationship between them, I answer, "Her niece."

The old woman approaches, her stick striking the ground with each step. "Get out of here now," she demands. "You're trespassing on private property." She sneers as her eyes fall on the cuts we're wearing, and with the misguided arrogance that comes with age, spits out, "You're a bunch of criminals. I insist you leave."

Drummer's not a man you can order around. Lazily, he leans back against his bike. "You employed SD Construction. The SD stands for Satan's Devils, in case you didn't know. You are conducting business with our club. Just so happens we've a reason to check this place out. We take security seriously, and when alerted that someone was on the premises, we were on the case straight away. You can thank us later."

The last comment almost causes her to have conniptions. Her mouth opens and shuts, and her body judders in rage. Then she finds her backbone again. "Well, I'm here now. I'll deal with any miscreants."

With only a rise of his eyebrow, fully visible in the headlights still glaring from her car, Drummer challenges her. "You're prepared to meet an armed assailant intent on stealing from the house?"

"There's nothing left worth taking," she states fast, confirming my suspicion, she's sold anything of any value.

It's at that moment that a scream comes from inside the building behind us. Siobhan starts forward, waving her stick threateningly. "Leave this to me."

"Not fuckin' likely," Peg states. He marches forward, takes her by her arms, and steers her back to her car. He nods to the chauffeur. "Get her out of here."

"I'm calling the cops."

"You do that."

I've already had enough of the altercation. Leaving them to it and conveniently forgetting I've put everything down to my imagination, I swing/hop my way to the entrance and push inside. That Mouse, Drummer, Blade and Wraith are right behind me suggests that I'm not the only one who heard the scream that can only have come from Maeve, unless someone else is haunting this place. Standing in the hallway, I shout out, "Maeve?"

My voice echoes, mockingly bouncing off the empty space around me. I try again. "Maeve! Can you come to me? Follow my voice."

It's like the building is alive—walls seem to be moving, closing in all around. Whispers and murmurings reach my ears, but none of the voices are those of my brothers. Something compels me to ignore my companions and let the house lead me where it wants me to go, which is to the stairs. I climb them laboriously, swearing at the awkwardness of manoeuvring my crutches and bad leg. I almost slip in my haste to ascend and have to pause to regain my breath and balance.

"Maeve?" I call out again. Hearing sounds, I continue to move upward. It's on the second floor that I'm faced with several closed doors, but there's one in particular I feel drawn toward. I twist the handle of the door to Maeve's childhood bedroom, pushing it open as apprehension seeps into my bones.

"Thank fuck," I announce, as I see Maeve's figure standing in front of me. I step inside, reaching for her as her body shimmers, flickers, and disappears.

A hand lands on my shoulder, startling me. "Just me." Mouse's reassurance comes as he adds, "I saw her too, Brother. She's here in spirit, but not in the flesh."

He saw her, too? At this moment, I can't deal with the implications.

I can't cope with everything that's going on. My head is spinning, and pain throbs at my temples. "What the fuck does that mean?"

"She's still in the hospital, Hound," Mouse's steady voice sounds. "You must have seen an image that she's projecting."

This shit is way out of my realm of belief or understanding. I can only think Mouse is highly susceptible and is picking up on my delirium. Before my accident, I'd never experienced anything that wasn't one hundred percent real.

"My brain's fucked," I determine.

"Mine too?" Mouse asks with a slight chuckle.

Suddenly the scene in front of me flickers, and without another warning, Maeve is present in the room once again.

"Hound?" She races forward, crashing into me. I have to tense my muscles in my unbroken leg to stop us both from falling to the ground. With force, she hits me. I'm hard pushed to think she's anything other than here in the flesh. "Thank God you're here! It felt like I was in a never-ending nightmare and that I was never going to get out."

Substance or not, her trembling ignites the protective part of me. "You're okay, I got you." I wrap both of my arms around her, holding her tight.

"Who the fuck's Hound talking to?" Drummer snarls, his voice making me conscious that my brothers have now climbed the stairs and are on the second floor.

"Hound, Brother..." Peg's hand lands on my shoulder, giving a supportive squeeze, but I shrug him off. There are more important things to deal with.

"What's happening, darlin'?" I speak to the woman who feels so right in my arms, her figure fitting as though she'd been built for me. But I put that strange thought aside, concentrating on her trembling body, and trying to calm her down, repeating, "You're okay now. I've got you."

"Hound?" When I don't respond, one of my brothers adds, "Doesn't anyone think we ought to call for a medic?"

"Shut it, Blade," Mouse snarls. "Hound is fine. Leave him alone." As my hands smooth up and down Maeve's back, I glance around at him, only to see his nostrils flaring, and his eyes open wide. "Brothers, don't you feel there's an existential presence? Or a strange odour in the air?"

"I can smell rotten eggs," Drummer replies.

"Sulphur," Blade corrects.

"Get out of here now!" It seems Siobhan's chauffeur wasn't able to corral her into the car, as she appears, with her driver running behind her. "You've no business being here. I've called the cops."

I might be holding onto a woman whose physical form is lying elsewhere in a hospital bed, but I still have some wits about me. What other reason could Siobhan have for wanting us out of the house, unless there's something here that she doesn't want us to find?

"Jesus fuckin' Christ!" The unnaturally high-pitched scream from Blade is so unusual that it makes me spin around.

For a moment, my emotions are completely in tune with his as the shimmering image of a woman appears, gradually solidifying in front of my eyes. She's got the same colouring and eyes and could be the twin of the woman I'm holding. Adding two and two together, I come up with the answer that she might well be the mother of the woman I'm comforting, evidence added when the newcomer's face softens as it rests on her daughter.

My thoughts are confirmed when Maeve gasps, "Mom?"

The sound of furniture overturning shifts my focus. Swinging around, I see Siobhan has stumbled back and lost her balance, falling into a table. Is it wrong that I feel some satisfaction seeing her lying on her back, floundering like an upturned turtle?

There's nothing wrong with her eyes, though, or her mouth. "You're dead!" Siobhan cries out.

"So am I." It's a new voice, deep and somehow musical. At first, there's nothing accompanying it, then slowly another form appears.

Drummer's, "Oh fuck," Peg's gasp of horror, and Blade's sudden step back complement the new apparition.

But it's this form that has Siobhan screaming and covering her face with her hands. I recognise it immediately as Emerald, one of the participants in the X-rated display I'd been subjected to the last time I was in the house.

Except for the strangeness of the situation, deep in my gut, I know the ghosts haven't appeared to terrorise us. Instead, they seem intent on targeting Maeve's aunt, which they are doing a great job of. Siobhan scrambles backward to get away from them, while holding her hands over her face as if to deny what she's seeing.

I stiffen. The appearance of Emerald has triggered a memory in my brain and planted a seed of excitement in my head. Something so imperative I just have to act on it now. While my companions are distracted, probably trying to come to terms with seeing spirits from beyond this world, while nothing now would surprise me, I take Maeve's hand and rush her out of the room.

As I approach her gramma's bedroom, Maeve hangs back, her head shaking rapidly side to side. "I don't want to go in there again."

The overwhelming sensation that I have to do this has me tugging at her hand. "I won't let anything hurt you." I hope I say it convincingly, but a loud rumble of thunder rattling the house unnerves me. *Is it a warning not to go inside?* Dismissing that notion, having a whole-hearted belief it's the right thing to do, I follow my gut and continue on.

Ignoring the other doorways, stepping over the gaping holes in the floorboards—one in particular proving a challenge for my crutch, needing me to leave my fragile masculine side behind momentarily—I accept Maeve's hand to help me over it. The door to my destination is closed, and I hesitate before opening it with my hand hovering over the knob, unsure if I want to see it in its current derelict state or in all its magnificence as I'd seen it before. My hand at the ready to hide Maeve's eyes from any ghost peepshow, I pluck up the courage, turn the handle, and expose the room behind the door.

There are no ghosts here, kinky or not. The room stinks of musk, the furniture covered in dust and cobwebs. Only the frame of the bed remains. Bird droppings cover the floor, and a bat swoops close by before ascending and disappearing via the hole in the ceiling that must lead to the upper floor. I clasp Maeve tight as she squeals and ducks her head.

"I don't like this," she confides.

I eye the dressing table that had been here before, but the elegance has faded, and it still lies shattered and discarded on the floor. The delicate wood inlays can still be seen on the surface, along with dust and fingerprints galore. The main drawer lies open and discarded. *It's obviously been searched.* Feeling downcast for a moment, I surmise whatever I expected has probably long gone.

Not ready to give up just yet, I close my eyes for a second, delving into the vision I'd had, the one I'd tried so hard to forget, of Bertie approaching the dressing table and how he made the hidden compartment appear. As I recall the details, I open my eyes once more and see, while toppled and drawerless, that part of the furniture is still relatively untouched. My heart rate speeds up in anticipation. *It can't be that easy, can it?*

I don't let go of Maeve's hand as I approach the once handsome antique. Keeping hold of her with my left hand, I twist my right into the space where the drawer used to sit, and try to find the mechanism Bertie surely triggered that night.

"What are you doing?" she asks, her voice steadier now we're alone.

"I don't fuckin' know," I reply, frustrated that I can't feel a button or anything. I'm now glad I hadn't raised her hopes. But I'm loath to give up. Trying again, I squeeze my fingers together and push in further.

I can feel something. Wincing as the wood compresses my fingers, I reach as far as I can. Then suddenly, *click,* and a secret compartment is exposed.

Beside me Maeve gasps, and I, too, hold my breath as I draw out what I've found, an amazing array of an elaborate emerald necklace, brooch, earrings, bracelet, and ring. I'm no jeweller, but I'm sure they must be worth a fortune. While the woman at my side is marvelling at the treasures I'm holding, my eye is caught by papers bound in ribbon that have fallen to the floor. Quickly passing the jewels to her, I reach down and pick them up. Smoothing the documents flat, my eyes are immediately caught by the title page. *Last Will and Testament of Emerald Sullivan.* Quickly, I flick through the papers, easily making sense of the meagre contents. She left the whole estate and all her worldly possessions to her granddaughter, Maeve.

Pulling Maeve closer, my voice is an octave higher than normal. "The house is yours. The jewellery too." Excitedly, I point to the document, my tone taking Maeve's attention away from the shimmering jewels. "Siobhan never had rights over any of this."

"Give that to me!" a deranged voice screams.

Seeing it's Siobhan standing in the doorway holding a gun, I spin, putting Maeve behind me. I notice her aunt's hand is shaking and unsteady, never a good sign with what I have to assume is a loaded weapon.

She advances a pace, and I step back, taking Maeve along with me, wishing like hell I'd come armed. But I'd been prepared to meet with ghosts, spirits and ghouls, not a flesh-and-blood enemy. I wonder why I was so worried earlier, when it's now that I'm facing the real danger.

"Give me the emeralds and that will," she snarls, still holding the gun in both her hands. "Throw them to me. They're rightfully mine."

"Not what this says," Maeve says from my rear, her hand reaching around me to point to the new will.

"Pah." Siobhan snorts. "Emerald said she'd changed her will when she believed the pack of lies Sian told her. She luckily died before she could file it. I've wasted all this time trying to find the updated version, then decided it was better to demolish the house so the will would be destroyed." She takes another step forward, madness blaring from her eyes. "I tried to burn the house down, but the fire wouldn't catch. I tried to get contractors to knock it down, but none wanted the job after they made an inspection. I've waited for far too long to get what I'm owed, so give me that will now, along with the jewels!" Her voice has risen so high, she's screeching. "I don't give a damn if I have to kill you to get them, and I'll take that damn paper as well."

Suddenly, I feel a chill seeping through my bones, and I shiver as though I've been shoved into a refrigerator. Maeve wraps her arms around me, probably in an effort to keep us both warm. A wind blows in even though the windows are closed, and dust swirls up, spinning in ever-quickening circles until it forms an almost solid wall between us and her. Suspecting it's not enough to stop bullets, I don't lower my guard.

The dust packs together so tightly it forms a figure. Then colours appear, the dress covered in peacock feathers, the body of Emerald taking form just after.

"No!" Siobhan shouts. Wryly, I focus on the gun in her hand, especially seeing her finger tighten on the trigger. "You're not real." I take her distraction to move Maeve further back out of her sight.

Then another figure appears beside Emerald. It's Bertie, and fuck me, he actually turns and gives me a wink. In a low voice, he addresses me. "Knew you'd been paying attention when you saw us. Knew you'd know where to look."

Christ! It seems ghosts have a sense of humour as it dawns on me their erotic show had been to imprint this room on my mind so I would know where to find the jewels when I came back.

The Emerald I'd seen before had been absolutely gorgeous, a beautiful face and a figure that would leave no one in any doubt why Bertie had had to have her. Now she starts to contort, the peacock feathers turning black, and a red aura surrounding her features. After his words to me, Bertie, too, begins to change, his form transforming into a huge, threatening monster.

"You disappointed me," Emerald roars, rising a foot off the ground as she does. "You lied and betrayed the Sullivan name."

"You tell her, Mother." I think we all jolt as Sian arrives at the door. Siobhan swings around, and while distracted, Bertie's ethereal arm elongates and removes the gun from her hand. That it drops by my feet is probably a coincidence, but I waste no time taking it into my possession.

"You robbed my daughter, sent her out on her own in the world when she was barely more than a child." Sian now appears beside her mother. *What the fuck is it with this family, as honest to God, she looks at me, and just like her father, she closes and quickly reopens one eye.* Her image flickers, then appears much younger, and hell, she's the spitting image of her daughter. That's not the only change. The room has once again transformed back to its former glory.

Just as I'm wondering how this is going to play out, Bertie's black shadow finger rises up, pointing at Siobhan. "Did you never wonder why you couldn't destroy this house? It was because of the true legacy that was within it. The real inheritance you tried to rob from my granddaughter."

Siobhan actually spits at him, then gives a demented laugh. "This house, despite your efforts to keep it standing, is falling apart around us. She has no fucking inheritance left."

Emerald cackles and backs up her husband. "The house was never worth anything more than what it meant to us. It only stayed standing to protect the treasure held within. It's the emeralds that have the real value. As you well know. You've spent your life trying to get a hold of them one way or another. Do you really think I missed you sneaking around, prying into the drawers and closets all under the pretence you were looking out for me?"

"They're mine. I deserve them." Siobhan's not backing down. She tries to charge through the ethereal figures in front of her, only to find they form a solid barrier.

"You're going to hell for all the lies you told." Bertie and Emerald stand arm in arm, now less human than demon as they stare at their errant daughter. Fire seems to burst from their eyes like laser beams. Expecting the worst, I turn my body and pull Maeve in hard against me, burying her face against my chest while keeping my eyes locked in her aunt's direction. Light flares, Siobhan screams, and a blue flame seems to consume her. She dances a death dance, her voice growing ever more shrill as the fire grows fiercer, then drops to the floor. Smouldering ashes are all that remain, and after a minute, as I watch dumbfounded, even those disappear, leaving not a mark on the floor.

CHAPTER SEVENTEEN
MAEVE

One minute, I was lying in a hospital bed, having extracted myself yet again from a nightmare, finding the familiar bleeping of the machines and soothing reassurances from the nurse more comforting than annoying. Then, suddenly, it was like I blinked, and once more a whirlwind sucked me away.

With my head spinning, I opened my eyes and couldn't believe the man of my dreams, Hound, was there. And then my mother and grandmother, whom I adored, appeared right in front of me. Only they're ghosts, spirits or conjurings of my imagination. Peculiar sensations have hold of me. I'm here. I can feel Hound holding me, yet some other part of me tells me it's not real.

If this is a dream, it's so damn vivid I must be going crazy.

Like a voyeur, I watch the scenes play out, men, who I've not met before are stunned into silence by the apparitions, the appearance of Siobhan, then Hound leading me away. I felt the apprehension when he wanted to take me into the heart of the house, my gramma's bedroom.

What followed struck me mute. Finding the emeralds, then the will, then being faced with a gun, which Hound took to be a real threat. And though Hound had tried his best to shield me from the horror, I'd seen my aunt burned to cinders by a supernatural flame. I should have been distraught. She was the only family I had left. But if I'm honest, I have to admit that I never liked her. Maybe deep in my brain, I hated her. Perhaps it had been my thoughts that had summoned up such a nasty end. Especially if she had robbed me of my inheritance.

If what transpired is actually real, I wouldn't have had to leave, to strike out on my own when I was just eighteen. While owning a place like this would probably have been too much for my young head, I wouldn't have been thrust out in the world without anything. Those jewels themselves would have set me up for life.

Maybe it's that I'm in shock having seen what's just happened to Siobhan, but my own life flashes before my eyes. Me, a Greyhound bus, an unknown town. No money, begging, and, a secret I'm barely able to admit to myself, letting my body be used by strangers just to be able to get by, numb while grieving the loss of all the family I'd ever had. Then, a hundred to one chance, finding a shelter that really wanted to help girls like me. The one benefit I'd had was that I'd graduated high school with a GPA of 4.0, which meant I was an oddity among the other girls the place was trying to help. They took me on as a sort of protégée. With their support, I enrolled in trainee courses and eventually secured a job that sponsored me to apply to business school.

I was one of the lucky ones. For a long time, I focused only on work, didn't socialise much, and certainly didn't want a relationship. My only forays into having sex had been those with a monetary reward. Once I could afford it, it took a ton of therapy for me to even step foot into the dating world, and a lot of time passed before I realised there was pleasure in sexual intimacy.

My caution, though, ensures I'm still single at the age of thirty-three. It wasn't my physical experiences that stopped me from getting in deep with anyone. It was the knowledge that, in the end, everyone leaves me. What's the point of giving my heart to someone if it was only to be broken?

This must be the worst fucking nightmare of my life, getting what-could-have-beens taunted in front of me. It must be a dream. It can't be anything more. I expect at any moment to get the sudden urge to pee, only to find there's no bathroom available to me. But the seconds tick by, and I don't feel the frantic need to find somewhere to relieve myself. Instead, I feel anger burn inside me.

My life would have been so different if Siobhan hadn't lied. *Her death shouldn't have been as quick as it had been.*

An urgent beeping sound fills my ears. I feel a tug as if a force is trying to take me somewhere I should be. *Thank God I'm waking up.* But the sound and feeling fade, and Hound's hand is on my arm, grounding me.

I suddenly realise, while I'd been lost in my head, the dream resumes in front of me. The scene in front of me has changed. The ghosts have disappeared, the room now missing all the elaborate furnishings. It's grown dark. Lightning flashes outside the window, the odour of sulphur is in the air, and the house groans ominously. In front of us, a beam crashes down, making Hound pull me back.

"What the fuck's happening?"

"Place is fuckin' falling down, Drummer," Hound yells back. "Get yourselves out of there."

"Not without you, Brother."

"Prez. Get out of here now!" Hound sounds angrier than

I've ever heard him. "I'm ordering you as your sergeant-at-arms."

There's more clattering as plaster falls around us. Ignoring the roar of protest coming from just down the corridor, Hound takes the emeralds from me, places them in his pocket, then secures the will in his jacket. He takes my hand. "We've got to get to the stairs."

I'm in no disagreement. Dream or nightmare, I'm unable to wake up, and I'm driven to make some effort to save myself. I follow his lead and go out into the hall as he places his crutch on a floorboard, which cracks and shatters, luckily before he puts his weight on it. In one smooth action, he's anchored himself, turned, pulled me up, and swung me over the gap. While I'm still recovering, he uses his crutch much like a pole vaulter and gets himself over as well. His barely smothered grunt suggests he'd put more weight on his injured leg than he's supposed to.

But with more banging, creaks and groans, I'm worried the house is going to implode around us, so it's me who now takes the impetus, pulling him forward toward the stairs. The men who had accompanied Hound have already reached them, and Hound shoos them away.

"Get the fuck out of here, Brothers."

Checking behind them as if to ensure we're following them closely, they descend fast, their boots sounding like a herd of buffalo as they race down the steps. It's our turn. We reach the top... then the whole staircase disintegrates in front of our eyes. Hound's momentum almost sends us both crashing down, but he drops his crutch, grabs hold of the newel that still stands with one hand, and wraps the other around my waist, pulling me back tight against him. My heart rate's beating as fast as I can feel his thumping against my back.

Below us, I see Hound's companions who'd waited. "Stay there," one demands.

"Just save yourselves," Hound roars.

As the men below disappear, I'm worried they've obeyed him at last. My only hope is that this is a nightmare, and that I will be able to wake up. Then realise, if I do, what will happen to Hound? *Unless he's just a figment of my imagination as well.*

Hound must realise the hopelessness of our situation as he turns me to face him. "Maeve, I'm so sorry." There's a hitch in his voice, and a flash of lightning shows the sadness in his eyes.

Placing my finger against his lips, I reassure him, "I wanted to come to this house." I even manage a strained chuckle. "Siobhan warned me how dangerous it was, but I disregarded what she said."

Hound puts both his arms around me when we stumble in unison as the house rocks. His intense eyes stare into mine. "I had an ol' lady once." When my brow furrows, he explains, "A woman, a partner. Thought she meant everything to me, but it didn't work out. Kind of spoiled me on the thought of relationships, until I met you." He pauses and throws his head back. His eyes close briefly, then he opens them again and looks back down. "I'm not even sure you're real, or if my injured brain has conjured you up. Though that seems too much of a stretch. If I drew a picture of my ideal woman, I couldn't have come close to what you actually are. You're everything I want, Maeve."

There's another crash, making us both jump.

It's time for me to be honest, too. "This can't be real, as you're the man I'd always dreamed of meeting. Too out of my league for me to do anything else but admire from afar in real life."

For a beat of time, we're still as statues, neither daring to breathe, then his mouth crashes down on mine and I experience the sort of kiss I've only read about in fiction. The last time our lips met, it was amazing. This time unbelievably tops that.

His hand cups the back of my neck, pulling me close as his lips devour mine, his tongue invades, and I damn near lose my mind. Everything about him assaults my senses—his natural perfume, his taste, the sound of his muffled groan as I return his kiss, and the feel of his warmth surrounding me.

Then he gets more demanding, his dominance turning me on. My core clamps as a rush of arousal floods through me, stronger than I've ever known. I feel him harden against me, instinctively moving closer and wantonly rubbing myself against him.

This isn't me. I've never been with such a dominant man before. Sex was either contractual when I turned my mind off, or polite and gone through as a necessity. I've never felt the impulse to hoist my leg around a man's thigh, to rub against him, the desire to get myself off taking over every part of me. But that's what I do now.

Without a word, he understands me. One hand still around my neck anchors my mouth to his, while the other takes hold of my leg and presses me tight to him, helping me get into a rhythm.

I'm so turned on, the illicit thought I shouldn't be doing this instead of turning me off, urges me on. As he presses his fully clothed hardness against me, I continue to rock. The house crashing around us fades into obscurity.

"That's it, baby. Give it to me," he encourages, as I plead with him with my eyes.

And heaven help me, but I can't stop the sensation that overtakes me, as I masturbate on his leg, then come, harder than I ever have before. I scream through my release. He swallows the sound with his mouth, still rocking against me, gently bringing me down.

He's staring at me as if I've just hung the moon for him.

Beep. Beep. Beep.

I try to hold on to him, but I'm clutching at air. My eyes stay fixed on his face, but it shimmers and disappears.

CHAPTER EIGHTEEN

HOUND

One minute I was holding a satisfied Maeve in my arms, dick throbbing in pants that had become far too tight for me, and then the next, I was holding air. While I'm still trying to process that, Drummer is shouting up the stairs.

"Hold on, Hound. We're coming for you."

"Just leave me, get out of here." With Maeve's disappearance, my worries about a debilitating brain injury have returned in force. I don't want anyone risking their lives to save this miserable one of mine.

But wanting and getting are two different things, as someone has somehow found a ladder and has placed it in the gap that was once the stairwell. It's Mouse who climbs up, reaching out his hand.

"I've got you, Brother. I'll help you down."

I shake my head, but his dark, almost mesmerising eyes fix on mine. It's as if he's in my head, telling me not to give up. While I don't want to live feeling I've lost my mind, some sense of self-preservation overrules any instinct other than to strive to survive. Picking up my crutch, I show it to him in warning, and he leans to one side as I throw it down.

Getting a one-legged man down a ladder isn't easy, but Mouse is determined. I take one step down, then lean back, trusting him to take my weight as he moves himself to the next rung. We then repeat the laborious action. It seems like it takes an eternity before Peg's strong hands come around my waist, lifting me the last couple of feet until my good leg can balance on the floor, and Blade thrusts my walking aid into my hands.

In the beams of their flashlights, I see Wraith pushing Drummer. "Let's get out of this fuckin' place."

Blade follows his prez and VP, and with Mouse's arm tight around me, I hop my way after them.

The noise around us is horrendous. The gentle moans of a dying house have crescendoed until there are screams protesting years of neglect. From everywhere come the splintering sounds of glass breaking and shattering on the ground, and a roaring like thunder, as wooden beams collapse. Dust swirls up, making it almost impossible to see, but somehow we all find our way unerringly to the entrance as if being drawn by some hidden string.

Kicking the door open, Drummer's first outside. We follow, and without discussion, put as much distance as we can between us and the house. Then, at the perimeter of what was once a well-tended garden, we turn in unison.

"Fuck!" Wraith exclaims.

"Will you look at that?" Blade asks.

"Thank fuck we got out," the ever-predictable Peg says.

"Even Bullet couldn't do a demolition job that neat," Drummer observes.

Mouse murmurs something in a language I don't understand, as we all stand watching as the house implodes, collapsing in on itself, until bricks, glass, and woodwork lie in a heap on the ground.

It's me who finally breaks the ensuing silence. "Guess that settles the question whether it's a recondition or demolition job."

I didn't expect the ensuing laughter, but perhaps I should have. It's a return to normality, a way of releasing pressure. Peg chortles loudly, Blade snorts, Drummer bends over, clutching his belly as he lets his mirth out.

Even Mouse is chuckling and slapping me on the back. "Good one, Bro."

"Hey, would you look at that?" Drummer, having recovered, states, gaining our attention. His voice is full of wonder as he points toward the east.

I, like the others, look in the direction where the sun is starting to appear behind the mountains. It's dawn, which must mean it's near seven o'clock in the morning. Halloween has now come and gone. *Thank fucking, God.*

All of a sudden, phones start going off all around.

"Hey, Sam. Yeah, I'm fine. Heading home now."

"Tash? I'm good. See you soon."

"Darcy, I'll be back before you know it."

"Sorry I left the horses to you, will make it up to you, Mariana."

In direct contrast, my phone stays dead in my pocket as one by one my brothers reassure their old ladies, obviously concerned that they'd been out of communication all night.

In age, I'm between the F.O.G.s and the young guys who now run the show. But even Hawk, Throttle, and Wizard have something I don't have. Not for the first time, I regret not having an old lady to call my own.

My head summons up a vision of Maeve, knowing she could have been my ride or die, but she wasn't real, and our interactions were only in my damaged head. I beat my fist against my forehead, wondering how it was possible to feel such a loss at something I never had.

"Time to get back to the compound!" Drummer waves his hand in the air.

Blade hesitates, casting a look at the remains of what once was a house. "Aren't we going to talk about this?"

"Not here," Peg says fast. "Maybe later. Though this is something I don't think I'll ever get my head around."

Drummer huffs softly. "Not sure it won't just be Hound needing his damn brain examined."

Maybe I could take some comfort that I didn't hallucinate everything alone. Unless, even this has been just another Groundhog Day Halloween, only in my mind. Though the presence of my brothers makes that hard to believe.

But something's missing. There's no Maeve. If this is reality, I think I'd rather lose myself in a fantasy where she could be here with me.

"Let's ride," Drummer insists again.

Around me, my brothers don't hesitate to obey him, heading to their bikes.

"Come on, Hound." Mouse takes hold of my arm and supports me across the rutted and uneven ground until we get to the SUV.

It's him having to help me that makes me feel completely useless, and though I'd describe myself as a card-carrying red-blooded man, tears prick behind my eyes. The only woman I ever felt a real connection with was summoned up by my broken brain.

"Snap out of it," Mouse growls as he puts the vehicle in drive. "Lost sight of you, but I sensed that there were spirits all around. If you saw things, I, for one, would believe they were truly there with you."

For a moment, I let my suspicions overtake me, that if I admit to him who was there, what I saw, and what went down, he'd use that as ammunition to take my patch from me. But there's something in his tone, or rather, something that's lacking. There's no judgment, no levity, just an acceptance that he'd believe whatever I said that I saw.

"I think I saw Maeve," he adds, gently.

Turning to him sharply, I question, "Really?"

There's a slight up-and-down movement to his chin. "Of course, it could have been me picking up on something you were projecting, but something was happening in that house for sure." He barks a laugh. "Houses don't just demolish themselves."

And that's the part no one had wanted to talk about once we'd escaped the ruins. He casts a sly look my way. "And in no sense was that in your head, Brother. That was something we all saw."

It's his quiet recognition that I've experienced things outside the norm that has me tapping my pockets and not finding them empty. With open eyes, I bring out what I find.

He risks a glance away from the road ahead, seeing the glint of the exceptional jewellery. His eyes go so wide, he swerves the car. After he's corrected the steering, he snaps out, "What the fuck, Hound?"

"Emerald's jewellery," my clipped voice explains. "Hidden in the remains of a dressing table." I swallow the lump in my throat and admit, "I wouldn't have found the secret drawer, wouldn't even have looked for it, if spirits hadn't shown me where to search." Before he can think I'm a thief, I add quickly, "They belong to Maeve."

"And that?" he asks about the documents I've next pulled out.

"The last will and testament of Emerald Sullivan, leaving

everything to Maeve. Siobhan never had any right to the house." I pause, then add, "Siobhan was there. The ghosts killed her."

As I glance at him, I see the rapid shake of his head. "Siobhan never entered. The chauffeur drove her away."

"She came back," I insist. "She's dead."

Then, in a manner I'd expect only from him, and from none of my other brothers, he shrugs nonchalantly and says, "Maybe the ghosts took revenge on her spirit, but she could still be alive in human form." He nods toward the paperwork I'm holding. "I'd guard that with your fuckin' life if I were you, Hound."

"And the jewels." I raise and dip my head in agreement. "It was them she'd been searching for." Out of the side of my eye, I see his jaw clenching. "I think we should go straight to the hospital to see Maeve." The jewels give me hope that while I might have been hallucinating her presence in the house, the woman herself is real – even though I clearly recall seeing her in a hospital bed, even that I could have dreamt up. A kernel of excitement bubbles within me. Could there be a chance that we could have a relationship after all? Or is that more of my damaged brain's fucked-up thinking?

"It's only just dawn. Way too early for visiting time, and," he casts a look at me, "you look awful, Hound. You're mentally and physically exhausted, and you're not the only one." He makes a show of stifling a yawn. "We'll head back, catch forty winks on the compound, and as soon as you wake, I'll take you to her."

Not what I want to hear. I want to get the jewels and will to Maeve while they still feel real. A large part of me thinks there's a possibility that, if I let go of them, they'll turn to dust. *But Mouse has seen them.* Or, at least, he's pretended he has. Maybe he's just pandering to my delusions. No. He saw them.

He asked about them. Now back in my pocket, I clasp my hand around them, using their solidity to ground myself, to prove to myself, not everything in the damned Sullivan House was an illusion.

Mouse hasn't lived on the compound for decades. Once he married Mariana, they took over a horse farm and made it their home, along with their four children. He no longer has a room put aside for him. He'll have to make do with a crash room if he's going to rest. I have many reasons to be grateful for him, for standing beside me and driving me around, and not immediately dismissing all the crazy things I've been saying. I make the offer.

"Want to catch a couple of hours' sleep in my spare room?"

His grin shows that he's grateful for the offer.

The sun is now balanced on the horizon as we park the SUV, and walking up the slope, we find the clubroom is quiet. Drummer and the others must have gone home to their old ladies, and while there should be a prospect keeping watch inside, everyone else will probably still be in their beds.

When we reach my house, I try to go through the motions of being a good host, offering food or drink, but I give up as he waves me off, just wanting a glass of water and then goes to crash and sleep.

Sustenance, whether liquid or solid, doesn't interest me either. I run through the shower, thankful to get all the dust and soot off me, and eye my bed. Instead of going to it, I dress in fresh clothes.

I'm antsy and on edge. While I know I might be turned away before visiting hours, I can't stay here. I need to get to Maeve now. For the sake of my sanity, if nothing else, and to reach her before the jewels and will disappear.

Opening the door to my house, I step out and then come to an abrupt halt.

"Didn't think you'd be able to wait, Brother." Drummer steps away from where he'd been leaning against the wall, his hand covering his mouth to hide a large yawn.

Fuck this. I growl at my temporary prez, "I need to go see her."

He snorts. "You mean the woman that you say was there last night? The one you saw but no one else did?"

I was about to push him out of my way, but the implications suddenly hit. *If he hadn't seen her last night... If he thought I was having conversations with someone he couldn't see...* Well, fuck. I've probably demolished any chances of regaining my rank or even staying a Devil.

As my mouth gapes, he smirks and shakes his head. "Right now, I'm reckoning you're thinking I'm going to accuse you of being fucked in the head." His raised eyebrow demands a response, so I cautiously lower my chin, then raise it. "Bro, I've seen shit in my time, but nothing like what I experienced last night. Apart from giving Mouse a pass due to his heritage, I'd have said everything on earth was black and white." He gives a lopsided grin. "Thought I was too old a dog to learn new tricks, but fuck, what I saw wasn't normal, wasn't natural, and I've no explanation to offer." This time his prompt to me is to lean his head to one side and widen his eyes as he looks at me.

Reaching into my pocket, scared in case I find they're no longer there, I pull out the jewels and show them to him. "I found these, as I think I was expected to. They belong to Maeve, always did, always will." I then take out the documentary proof and pass it to him. "Siobhan never had any rights to that house." Straightening my spine, going for gold, thinking he's bound to call the men in white coats to come put me in a straitjacket and take me away, I risk it all. "The house held secrets. Siobhan couldn't get rid of it, couldn't sell it, and it failed to catch light when she tried to burn it down. These jewels and the will were kept safe and sound until they could be placed in the hands of the right person." I add the clincher. "Siobhan went into the house and didn't come out." Again, that quizzical brow rises. "She was killed." I brush the hair back from my face. "By Emerald and her man."

"Brother." Stepping close, he places a hand on my shoulder. Drawing in a shuddering breath, I realise my time has come. He's got to kick me out of the club. He can't have a madman in it. "I saw enough, but not half as much as you." His sympathy undoes me. *He sounds like he believes me.* But he can't, can he? He grins and nods down at the jewels, "You need to get those items you found into the right hands. And I'm curious enough to come with you."

"Ain't going alone." Wraith suddenly appears from wherever he'd clearly been eavesdropping. He grins widely at me. "I'm tired as fuck, but last night was the best fun I've had in years. I'm not going to miss out on solving the rest of this mystery."

Nosy fucking bastards.

It doesn't help that on the way into Tucson, my current prez and VP converse quietly together, though not low enough to be unable to hear every word they say. The reason they want to come with me? To see Maeve for themselves and to see if she recognises me.

It makes me even more on edge when we arrive at the hospital. Even though I visited before, I truly can't say whether that was real or in a dream.

CHAPTER NINETEEN
MAEVE

"Good to see you back with us," the nurse cheerily pronounces as I open my eyes.

After her declaration, she focuses her attention on reading my outputs that appear on the screen. At the same time, I try to come to terms with the fact that I'm no longer in the Sullivan House, that Hound's arms are no longer around me, and that apart from the beeps of the machines, there are no sounds. No crashes of thunder, no creaks, sighs, or bangs, and no house collapsing in on itself.

It's hard to ground myself as my head spins. It doesn't help when the nurse turns her attention back to me, shining a light into my eyes, making me flinch. Then, stepping back, she grins reassuringly. "All seems good, Ms. Sullivan. The doctor will be in to see you shortly."

Is it wrong that my focus isn't on my health, but on the experience I'd just been living? If it was only a dream, it's the most powerful one I've ever had in my life. I can't imagine why I remember it so well and so clearly, in technicolour as well. I recall smells, feelings, sounds, as well as sight.

Common sense tells me I'm here in the hospital, and that I've never left. Maybe the drugs they've been giving me have had me hallucinating. I've not been anywhere, except in my head. I'm vaguely impressed at how my brain can manufacture situations and people in such detail.

These are the facts. A dream drove me to want to visit the home where I spent most of my teenage years, a desire so imperative I couldn't ignore it. On the way to Tucson, my car was totaled. I'm lucky to be alive. It's probably the morphine I've been given that has caused these vivid imaginings. I'll just have to get the medical staff to back off the painkillers, then maybe my brain will come to rights.

Or give me more. If under the drug's influence, I conjured up someone like Hound, who makes my body come alive and sing, why wouldn't I want to go back there again? Though didn't I meet him in real life when he visited me in hospital? Or was even that a dream? I don't know what's truth or fiction, but oh, how real those emeralds had felt in my hands. Maybe once I'm out of here, I'll see if I can turn my hand to writing fiction. My brain obviously knows how to summon up stories.

Resting my head back on the pillows, I try to relive my dream once again. Unlike so many others, I can recall every detail. How Hound came to the hospital, along with his Native American friend. How he'd saved me, not once, but twice, and how I disappeared when we were just getting to the good part, even if it was in a rapidly disintegrating house. My face flushes as I remember his touch. *It was all too real.*

But it can't be. I'm sure the nurses would have noticed if I'd been walkabout. I didn't meet ghosts, watch spirits kill my despicable aunt—while what happened was all in my head, that there was another will she'd been trying to find or ultimately destroy does explain a lot. I wouldn't put that past her.

My thoughts are interrupted as a man in a stereotypical

white coat appears, stethoscope hanging around his neck—a thoroughly useless bit of kit now, as the machines I'm hooked up to give him all that information without a need to get close. He's wearing a serious expression.

"Ms. Sullivan," he begins, his eyes narrowing as he gets a closer look at me, then up at the statistics on the screen display. "Your heart went into atrial fibrillation. We needed to perform a cardioversion to get it back into normal rhythm."

While that sounds serious, I'm here, I'm breathing, and I actually feel better than I have for days. I no longer feel sleepy, and I no longer have that persistent throbbing in my head. There's only one thing I want to know now. "When can I be discharged?"

His brow furrows. "I don't think you understand. The injuries caused by the crash shouldn't have affected your heart. You need to stay while we run tests and find out the underlying causes. I can't in all good faith discharge you. If you hadn't been here and able to immediately receive our care, you would have been in trouble."

Now more compos mentis than I've been since I first awoke, practical worries start going around my head at the mention of tests. A long hospital stay is sure to be expensive, and I can only hope the driver who crashed into me was insured so I can recoup the expenses of the injuries he caused. The costs of investigating a hitherto unknown heart disease are surely going to be far more than I can afford. I have health insurance via my job, but even so, my co-pay is ridiculous. I *feel* fine. Better than I did before I passed out for the second time.

Hey, look at me. Even with the stress of dealing with the doctor's words and my worries about being able to afford them, there have hardly been any spikes in my blood pressure. Nor much of a rise in my heart rate. *I can read a monitor as well as anyone.* Not feeling at death's door, I fix my eyes on the doctor. "I want to leave. I'll accept it's against medical advice."

A deep sigh suggests he's been here before, and his eyes soften with what I interpret as sympathy. "I can't force you to stay, but I strongly advise it."

I throw him a bone. "I'll see my own doctor when I get home."

His jaw clenches. "If you have a heart attack, you might not survive."

I may be crazy, *but due to my detailed dreams, that's probably true; however,* I feel completely normal. "Nevertheless, I want to go home." There's my work, for one thing. I haven't been able to contact them up to now. All they know is that I took a week's leave and disappeared off the face of the earth. *Have I even got a job anymore?* I bite my lip as that thought adds more impetus to my wanting to leave.

He flinches. "You'll have to sign a document, agreeing you discharged yourself against medical advice." After I jut out my chin, my agreement obvious in my stance, he despairingly adds, "Just tell me you have someone accompanying you wherever you go. Who will be there to monitor and look after you, and get you medical attention the moment there appears to be something wrong?"

I hate lying, but sometimes situations call for the truth to be blurred just a bit. I summon the words, open my mouth to reassure him I won't be alone when another voice answers for me.

"I'll be taking care of her."

Just as I'd accepted that my dreams had been just that, the deep tones of the man whom I shouldn't know cause my head to swing round. "Hound?" I gasp, drawing in air sharply. "You're real?" *It can't be, can it? I can't be faced with the man who literally is right out of my dreams.*

His very solid-looking grin speaks volumes, along with his words. "In the flesh." He steps forward, taking hold of my hand, squeezing my fingers reassuringly. "I've got you, Maeve." His dark eyes focus on mine, deep meaning flooding out of them. "I've *always* got you." While his serious expression doesn't change, he winks at me. "You know I'll give you anything. I'll shower you in *emeralds* if that's what you desire." His brow rises.

My heart literally skips a beat, as evidenced by that damn monitoring machine, and my mouth gapes open as I stare at him. Giving an awkward glance toward the doctor, I see that he's stepped back a pace, eyes on my chart as if giving my visitor some space. I want to ask if he, too, can see Hound, but can't force out the words. If he didn't want me to leave the hospital, he's hardly going to be more encouraged if I admit I'm seeing people who aren't there.

As if cognisant of my confusion, Hound leans closer, speaking softly into my ear. "I don't understand it myself, but if you dreamed you were in the Sullivan House, then I was right there with you. And in my pocket, I've got the emeralds that belong to you, and the will that names you as the owner of the house..." he shrugs wryly. "Or at least, the land on which it once stood."

Then he stands back, as though waiting for my reaction.

Where the house once stood? I don't disappoint him. "It's gone?"

Again, he lifts then lowers his shoulders. "I think so. Or, at least, that's what I saw. Fuckin' place demolished itself."

Is it wrong that I don't care if what he says is true? Visiting the Sullivan House was the sole reason I came to Tucson, or was it? Maybe it was to find something else. Answers to questions that plagued my life.

A cough reminds us that the doctor is still here. "Ms. Sullivan, I'd like to request that your friend step out so I can talk to you privately."

My heart leaps. *He can see him.* As Hound gives me a wry look before turning to go, I grab for his hand, not wanting to take the chance of him disappearing again.

Knowing the doctor is likely to talk me out of leaving the hospital, I get in first, "I'd like to discharge myself now."

"Ms. Sullivan. I can't emphasise enough how important it is that you stay here and be monitored at the very least. At best, I want to run tests to find out the cause."

Hound squeezes my fingers again. "She'll stay for twenty-four hours," he announces for me, his eyes fixing on mine as if hoping I'll be okay with him taking over. "But after that, she's discharging herself."

The doctor's back straightens. "It's my utmost recommendation that she stays here for the next few days. Until we can be sure she's stabilised."

"My insurance won't cover it."

And it's that stark, believable statement that gets him to back down. He huffs. "As I said, you'll be discharging yourself against medical advice and will need to sign a statement to that effect."

Only a moment's doubt flickers through my mind. I'm convinced that against all odds and all reasonable explanations, my life and Hound's have become intertwined. That he'll keep me safer than any medical treatment can. And if not? I'd rather spend my last minutes, hours, or days exploring my attraction to this handsome and caring man than in a hospital bed wired up to machinery. The heat in his eyes and the memory, vision, hallucination, whatever of his hands touching me, makes me think there's nowhere else I'd rather die than in his arms.

Yeah, even a part of me thinks I've lost the plot and should be locked up to keep me safe and have the key thrown away.

Nothing, since I've returned to Arizona, has made any sense.

The doctor shakes his head, sighing heavily. "I'll see you in the morning and check your condition then." He leaves.

As he does so, two other men enter the room. Both sport wide grins. I notice Hound rolling his eyes.

"Couldn't wait, I see?"

"Brother, popped in to see Wiz, then came to be introduced to your woman."

My brow creases as they seem familiar. "Weren't you there last night?"

"We were," the brusque older man with salt-and-pepper hair and sporting an almost white beard replies. "But missed seeing you, Maeve."

Because I was only there in my head.

Squeezing my hand that he's still holding, Hound makes the introductions. "These are my brothers, Drummer, my prez, and Wraith, my VP." He narrows his eyes toward them. "Nosy fuckers just wanted to meet you."

Brothers? Adopted, maybe, but not blood. But what does that matter? Blood's turned me away all my life. At the edges of my memory, I recall Hound saying he belonged to a motorcycle club. But after everything that's been happening, that seems insignificant to me. They've not been the scariest people I've been faced with.

With a smirk toward Hound and a smile for me, Drummer turns to leave. "We'll see you back at the compound, Brother." He adds so quietly, I almost don't hear, "Now that we've seen she's real."

As the door closes behind them, letting go of my hand, Hound parks his ass in the uncomfortable visitor chair by the side of the bed, carefully placing his crutches within easy reach. "What are you doing?" My voice falters a little.

"Staying right here." His eyes focus on me and sharpen. "Don't understand one fuck of what's going on,but figure your life might be in danger. You need protecting, little dove."

"Dove?" I snort. Then I get to the main subject. "We both saw Siobhan die. You've brought me the evidence to get my inheritance..." For a second, doubt plagues my mind. "Haven't you?"

"Got it stored in a safe place," he confirms. Then he shakes his head. "But is Siobhan really gone? You and I both saw that in a dream, or perhaps in a different reality. Maybe it was the truth, maybe not. The only thing that's concrete is the emeralds and the original copy of the will. If Siobhan's still breathing, you're still at risk." He shrugs his shoulders. "You're now in possession of what she's been hoping to find for years."

Staring at him, I swallow, then swallow again. I open my mouth, shut it, grind my teeth together before parting my lips once more. "You think her death was an illusion?"

"Or wishful thinking," he offers. He chuckles, huffs, then opens his hands as if making an offering. "Not too damn sure how a brain-damaged man who sees things that aren't there can offer you protection, but, babe, I'll be fucked if I don't want to try."

Maybe I've always been drawn to the wrong type of men in my life, but no one's ever made the offer to keep me safe before. It warms something inside of me, and my apparently erratic heart starts to beat steadily at the idea of staying close to the one man who has.

My voice hitches as I say breathily, "Hound, lie beside me. I want to feel your arms around me."

He's been looking away, lost in his head, but my words cause him to turn sharply and look at me.

"Please?" I never expected to be begging this way.

But as soon as he hops over to the bed, sitting, then pulling first his good leg, then the broken one up after him onto the mattress, and I feel his arms surround me, I feel a security that it's been years since I've last felt, and a feeling that this is where I'm supposed to be.

CHAPTER TWENTY
HOUND

It's completely crazy. I'd felt a connection with Maeve the times that I'd seen her in my imagination, my dreams. But now she's in my arms, solid and real, I know I've finally found my one, that fate has brought us together. I can also tell that she's as confused as I am. Our world, since we met, has hardly been normal. Unreal, unbelievable are inadequate words for what's happened to us.

She holds onto me as though she's scared I might disappear, the same way she vanished on me, but I don't share her worries. I give any credence to the sixth sense I'm feeling. We've come to a junction in the road, where the spirits have gone, leaving us to our own devices, and whatever direction we take is up to us.

My mind is easier than it has been for days. I'm relaxed in a way that I've never been since first awaking from my accident. Although the odours of the hospital overwhelm almost everything, I can still sense her own unique perfume as I breathe in deeply against her skin, her natural pheromones drawing me in like a moth to the flame, already warning me I'm never going to want to let her go.

In other circumstances, I might find it annoying, but that rhythmic bleeping of the machine reassures me she's alive and she's here. Her breathing has gradually shallowed as she's drifted into sleep, but at least I have the audible confirmation that her heart's beating normally.

Despite the lights that still shine, albeit dimmed, and that I shouldn't find it possible to rest, I feel myself relaxing as I lie, holding her tight. My eyes close, my mind ceases its torment, and finally, for the first time in weeks, I drift off into a dream-less sleep. Until something has me snapping awake. It's someone entering the room. Expecting a nurse, I start to rehearse the reasons why I shouldn't be kicked out of her bed, out of the room, or even off the premises. But to my shock, she just shakes her head, does her checks, then, with a finger to her lips, creeps out of the door, closing it to give us some privacy.

After a while, Maeve wakes from sleep, her motion in turn arousing me. Turning my head, I see her staring into my eyes, a perplexed expression adorning her features. "Are you really here?" she asks.

"I'm here," I confirm, proving it with a gentle kiss to her lips. "Hell, Maeve, if you're wondering what's going on, you can't be more confused than me." Shaking my head, I grin. "Seems like most of our meetings have been on some spirit plane, or in some shared dream. Fuck, I thought I was going crazy."

"Same as me."

A buzzing sound disturbs us. I slide my phone from my pocket. Reading the text, I exhale deeply. Glancing at her face, I wonder how to tell her the news.

She's not stupid. My reaction has told her the words I've received involve her. "What is it?"

"Your aunt was found dead this morning, in her house. A heart attack."

She sucks in air. "So she's gone for real?"

Pulling her into my arms, I murmur, "Sure seems so. Mouse's information is normally right."

After being silent for a moment, she sighs. "I suppose it doesn't matter now what Gramma's intentions were. Siobhan sold anything of any value, and there's now no house."

"There's the land," I tell her. "And we've got the will."

"Wouldn't that be odd? A will turning up out of nowhere fifteen years after the testator died? There's no proof it's genuine."

Acknowledging she's got a point, I grimace, then come up with an idea. "We'll get our club lawyer to look at it. If it's out of her experience, I'm sure she'll know someone who can help. And we'll have to find out if Siobhan made arrangements before she died. If not, everything of hers should come to you as her only living relative."

Instead of showing her interest, she looks downcast. "I've no money for lawyers…"

"Babe." I chuckle. "You've got a fortune in jewels. Anyway, don't worry about it. Alex, our lawyer, will do it as a favour to me. She and Dart always love having an excuse to come visit Tucson." It's true. And we love it when their son Tyler comes along with them, now a patched Devil in the San Diego chapter himself. Goes by the road name Spark, and definitely has that about him. The kid occasionally visited when I was a prospect, always proud as fuck of the leather cut he'd been given with "Junior Prospect", or some such shit on the back. Apparently, they had to get him a new one every year, as once his illness was under control, he grew like a damn weed.

"Hound?"

"Yeah, babe?"

"Could you see if my purse is anywhere?" After a shake of her head, she continues, "I haven't thought of it before, but I need to see if my phone is here with me."

She doesn't have to ask twice. There's only one place where I suspect it would be. Eschewing my crutches for now, I bear my weight on my right leg, balancing my hands on the bed, and move around to look in the cupboard in her bedside table. Sure enough, there's a black shoulder purse there. When I pass it to her, she rummages and pulls out her phone.

Then sighs. "It's dead as a dodo."

Can't say I'm surprised. "Give it to me, and I'll try and find someone with a charger."

Instead of passing me the phone, she takes my hand, wrapping her fingers around mine tightly. "Don't go."

"Afraid I won't come back?"

Her eyes close, and a little shiver goes through her. "Something like that."

Getting myself back on the bed, lifting my useless leg, I pull her to me again. "This time you're not going to get rid of me so easily." But I can't say I don't understand her worry.

Our eyes catch. This time, it's her who makes the first move, gently placing her hand around the back of my neck, a slight raise of her brow to warn me of her intention, then she pulls herself up, leaning forward until our lips meet.

Her approach is almost teasing as her mouth moves on mine, an innocent kiss, but I let her play, hoping she'll take it further before I take charge. While I let her lead the caress, I can't help entangling my hand in that mass of red curls, breathing her in.

Exploration over, she pulls away with a chaste peck before raising her head and letting our eyes meet. I could drown in those pools of green eyes, her pupils enlarged, showing her arousal. Before I can move, this time she slams her lips down, her tongue licking at my seams until I open my mouth and let her in.

Her enthusiasm awakens something inside of me, and I can't help but take charge, rolling my body until I'm leaning as far as I'm able to on my side. With one hand in her hair, and the other against her waist, I pull her to me, so tight nothing separates us except the sheet that she's encased in.

Our kiss deepens, becomes more wild. Knowing this time no ghosts are going to stop me, I can't get enough of her taste or of her little moaning sounds. Who moves first, I don't know, but our bodies press harder together. My unruly cock is ready to go, but it doesn't scare her. She rubs herself against me. Our movements get more frantic as we dry hump each other, totally oblivious of anything else.

"Well, I..." The stranger's voice has us jumping guiltily apart. We turn as one to see a nurse standing, hands on her hips, a twist to her mouth as she regards the now fast beeping monitor and continues, "I guess I'm not going to have to trouble the doctor for your elevated heart rate, nor the flush to your face." She actually chuckles. "Honey, I think if I had such a fine specimen in my bed, I'd probably be in the same state."

Guilty like a school boy caught in a compromising position behind the bleachers, I immediately let Maeve go and start to disentangle my body from hers.

The nurse says, "You can stay where you are. At least while I'm on duty." Even though she'd dismissed Maeve's symptoms, she nevertheless steps forward to regard the monitor.

As my brows rise in surprise at her understanding, she explains, "Ms. Sullivan's not had many visitors the whole time she's been here. It's good to know she's got a boyfriend who cares about her."

"I care," I confirm. It's a dilution of what I actually feel for her, but Maeve is going to be the one who hears my true feelings first. Now's not the time or place for me to make any great pronouncement about how I want her as my old lady, maybe even my wife. For fuck's sake, I don't even know if she feels that way about me, though the reciprocal physical attraction is not in doubt.

"Nurse... Beckett?" Maeve peers to read her name tag. "Is there any way I could get my phone charged?"

"Sure." The nurse beams. "I'm sure I'll be able to find a charger. What type of phone?" When Maeve shows her, she nods and disappears.

I gaze after her. "She's nice," I tell Maeve. "My nurse was a troll."

"She's good people," Maeve agrees. "Do you think she'll let you stay the night with me?"

"No one's going to send me away," I reassure her, then smirk. "You think you can control your heartbeat if we kiss again?"

She casts an eye at the monitor. "It's annoying that I'm still hooked up."

It sure is. My cock deflates at the thought that anything we get up to will be broadcast around the hospital, or at least at the nurses' station. "Tomorrow," I tell her. "You're coming back with me, where no one can disturb us."

She intakes a breath. "I hadn't given any thought about where to go when I'm discharged. I thought I'd be heading home."

Her heart might be beating fast, but mine stops. "Where's home?" I snap.

"LA," she replies.

I roll onto my back. *Had she not even thought about staying with me?*

Picking up on my abrupt change in mood, she reaches for me. "Hound, this thing between us... I don't know what to do. I don't want to lose you, but I've got a job to get back to and responsibilities."

Oh fuck! I know nothing about her. "Husband? Boyfriend? Kids?" Then, remembering what the nurse said, think if she has another man, I'll hunt them down and kill them for not coming to Tucson to be with her.

She puts her hand on my arm. "Nothing like that. I'm completely single." As I let out a breath in relief, she continues, "We don't know each other at all. You don't know what I did to keep myself going when my gramma died and left me penniless, but I can tell you it wasn't pretty." She shudders. "If you knew I had to live on the streets and what I had to do to survive, maybe you wouldn't want me." My gut clenches as I read between the lines, but she doesn't give me a chance to answer her. "I was lucky. I was given a way out. I've never been in a relationship, as I've worked my ass off, never wanting to be destitute again. I've got a good job, and I owe everything to the people who gave me a chance. I don't want to let anyone down." She swallows, and I see her throat work. "I've got clients who've stayed with me for years, and they depend on me."

"What do you do?" It's an innocent question to ask, and one that solidifies how little I know about her. All I really know is I admire her character, her looks, and that her body was made for me. But I can't convince myself that if I knew more, it would make me want to walk away from her. Even the thought that she had to whore herself out means nothing to me. At least her reason was honest, to make money to live. What excuse have I got for the years when I fucked anything with a pussy, just because I could?

There's a spark in her voice as she answers. "I'm an accountant."

Well, fuck. Looks like she did make something of herself.

It's confession time. "I'm a biker. I'm a member of an MC." She nods as she already knows that. I grit my teeth. "The Satan's Devils still wear the one-percenter patch, the yellow diamond on our cuts, even though nowadays we earn our money honestly. But, babe, won't kid you, there are times we don't abide by citizens' laws, but only when there's a need to protect our own." I decide not to tell her about Road's track. I feel her tense, so I say quickly, "Our club is all about family. We've grandparents, parents, and kids. Hell, the second generation is heading the joint now. Drummer, who you met, well, his son is the VP." I try to make a hard sell. "We live in what was an old vacation resort. So much room, a lot of us have built our homes there. I've got my own house. You can come and live with me."

"Hound!" she barks, stopping my flow. "I've never been able to throw caution to the wind." As she glances at me, her eyes soften. "I've got deep feelings for you, but a deeper fear of things going wrong and me being left alone." Her head turns away as she says softly, "Everyone leaves me."

"Not me." I emphasise the words.

"I can't take the chance. Or, not immediately. Perhaps we could try a long-distance relationship…"

The door opening interrupts her. "Here's a charger!" the nurse announces triumphantly. She's even so helpful as to plug the phone into the socket and hand the now-charging device to Maeve.

"Thank you," Maeve tells her.

Taking her cue, the nurse leaves.

Picking up where we were interrupted, I ask, "Maeve, have you ever just lived?" As she goes to speak, I place my hand over her lips. "You were just a teenager when you learned you were going to lose your mom. Then, not long after she died, your gramma left you, too. Seems to me you've never had a chance to be free and just be. Why don't you…"

I've lost her attention as her phone beeps, coming back to life. She holds up a finger, indicating she wants me to be quiet.

Knowing it's useless for me to continue while she catches up with her life, I let her tap in her code, then shift to her emails. As she continues to read, I stare at the wall. I can't let her slip through my fingers. How can I convince her to stay with me?

"No!" she suddenly exclaims, throwing her phone down onto the bed. She places her head in her hands, and a sob comes from her mouth.

Guiltily, knowing I'm invading her privacy, I pick up the device and skim through the last email she was reading. In essence, it says she's exceeded her agreed-upon week's leave, has failed to contact her company despite numerous communication attempts, and therefore her employment has been terminated. *I deserve to burn in hell for the pleasure that sweeps through me.*

Though it goes against every part of me, I offer her hope. "They can't do this under the circumstances. You were in a coma. Once they know, they'll reconsider. We'll get Alex onto this as well."

She rallies. "You're right. I'll message back and explain." And now I have to try to be supportive as she types out a lengthy reply. By the way she's biting her lip, I can tell she's choosing her words carefully, and making her case as best she can. Then she says the words that send a dagger right into my heart. "I can't afford to lose my job, Hound. My whole life's in LA."

Her life's in LA. She speaks as though there's nothing for her here. As though the connection we feel is nothing. Although today's been the first real interaction we've had, I feel that through everything we've experienced, the horrors, the supernatural, people returning from the dead, the thought we could have been facing death together meant as much as having spent a lifetime with each other. What does it matter what background you have or where you grew up, when you've got to know the deep inner essence of the person you're with? All the rest are niceties that can be learned in time.

Moments ago, she was afraid I'd disappear. Now it seems I've got no ongoing place in her life. I'm wishing that I could say I'm having a hallucination, but this is one nightmare from which I'll never wake up.

I thought she was my one.

She obviously does not.

Fuck it. I glance at her, but her attention's not on me. It's on that fucking email app on her phone. She's biting her lip and staring as though she can make a response appear with just her will. That the answer has become the most important thing to her is obvious as she doesn't seem to notice when I leave the bed, nor when I pull my crutches toward me.

"I'm going to go get something to eat."

She barely acknowledges my words, nor looks up as I leave.

CHAPTER TWENTY-ONE
MAEVE

Of course, the company doesn't respond immediately. I'm a fool to think they will. Nevertheless, that doesn't stop me from refreshing the app, hoping a new email will appear. Surely they'll understand and make allowances as to why I've been out of touch for so long? There was no one to contact them. The emergency contact listed on my medical records was my one living relative, Siobhan. When originally asked, I had no idea who else to name and had forgotten to change it since then. It shows what a sad person I am, that even now I can think of no one I could name in her stead.

Except for Hound.

Only, I glance around the room. He's left me. Or more truthfully, I drove him away. Throwing my phone down on the bed, I realise how stupid and unfair I've been. So intent on trying to keep my job, I hadn't realised how cold I was coming over to him. Sure, my drive to survive since I originally left Tucson was deeply ingrained in me. But what does a life mean without someone to share it with?

If my job is still open, what do I gain? I'll go back to my lonely existence, living only to go to work every day, feeling I'm contributing to the world by sorting out other people's finances. Accountants have a reputation for being boring, and that sums me up perfectly. My job and life in LA is safe. Stepping into the unknown, putting my happiness in someone else's hands, demands a leap of faith, one I'm not sure I'm strong enough to take.

Having met Hound, though, is survival enough? What would my life have in store for me were I to throw caution to the wind and stay in Tucson to see whether a relationship between me and Hound would work? Or, seeing that he's left me alone, have I lost the chance?

My scalp itches. Absent-mindedly, I scratch it, realising just how long it's been since I've taken a shower. Damn near four weeks in a coma, and I haven't been out of this bed. As I smooth my hands down the strands, I realise my hair's a tangled mess.

Hound never mentioned that.

Suddenly, I'm embarrassed. I must look like a total wreck. *Yet he still kissed me, held me, touched me as if I were his world.*

A new urgency rises, and I press the call button for the nurse. When she appears, I ask to be disconnected from the monitors so I can go to the bathroom and get tidied up. When she knows my mind is made up, she takes all the sensors off my body and helps me sit up. Then she steps back, her hands at the ready, as I gingerly stand up.

I feel as weak as a newborn foal as I shakily get to my unused feet. It takes a moment to get used to being upright, and I make my way toward the bathroom, balancing with one hand on the bed.

"Let me help you," she says, as I reach open space. I'm grateful for her supportive arms around me.

I didn't realise she was going to assist me in the shower, but even with the chair, I'm glad of her help, despite the loss of my dignity.

Clean again, I dress in a fresh hospital gown, having nothing else to wear—my clothes from the accident were cut off me and destroyed, and I've no idea what happened to my case, which had been in my car. My wet, but clean, hair hangs loose and heavy, and I'm grateful when she hands me a comb.

"So where's your man gone?" she asks conversationally.

Frowning, I bring back into my mind the last words that he said. "He's gone to get something to eat." An explanation simple enough that she accepts it without further comment.

It might satisfy her, but it does nothing for me. My head is in turmoil with numerous questions. Topmost, of course, is whether he'll be back. Or has he come to his senses and washed his hands of me? I certainly hadn't given him any encouragement to stay.

When she's happy I'm safely back on the bed, the nurse leaves. It's then that tears start to leak from my eyes, as I slowly pull the teeth of the comb through the wet strands of my hair. Even when all the tangles are removed, I keep up the motion, finding it hypnotic and comforting.

And all the while, the door to my room stays stubbornly closed.

The clock on the wall tells me an hour has passed, and then two. My hair's air-dried, I look more presentable, but my heart feels empty, as I wonder for whom.

He's given up on me. And who could blame him? He offered me a new life, and I showed no interest.

What do I want? That's the problem. It's never been a choice. I went to my gramma's as Mom was dying, and after her death, I was kicked out with nowhere to go. I've muddled through life doing things that I didn't want to do. A paid whore? Never wanted that, but it was necessary. I took the chance to study for my degree, and then accepted the first job offered because I was too afraid to do anything else. I've never been presented with alternatives as to where I could go.

Now I have, I'll try not to choose the wrong one. But maybe, I already have. I've let Hound go.

I know he's a member of the Satan's Devils' club. If he doesn't come back, maybe I could go and seek him out.

My hand covers my mouth as the realisation hits me. I don't actually give a damn about keeping my job in LA. A future with Hound is far more enticing. That is, if he gives me another chance.

When the door opens, I don't even look up, expecting the medical staff to be doing their rounds once again. But the gruff clearing of a throat gets my attention.

It's Hound in the flesh. For a moment, I'm so stunned, I can't get any words out. I must look like a fool with my mouth gaping.

He enters, that practiced motion with his crutches bringing him to the chair beside the bed, moving stiffly as if not sure of his welcome. His eyes examine me. "You look better."

Well, anything would be an improvement on how he last me. "I showered," I say, needlessly.

As a conversation starter, it falls flat. An awkward silence descends, then he takes in a shuddering breath, and nods at my phone that I've long forgotten, and which is lying where I left it at the foot of my bed.

He clears his throat, then asks hesitantly, "Have you received your employer's response?"

I'd honestly forgotten about it. "I don't know." As he raises his eyebrow, I take a deep breath. "I'm frightened, Hound. More scared than I was in the house. I don't want to go back to LA. I want to stay in Tucson and explore whatever this connection between us really is. But should I really burn my bridges, based on knowing you only for a few short hours while I've been awake?"

Earnest eyes stare in to mine. "What are you trying to say, Maeve? Do you want to stay or go? 'Cause one moment it sounds like you've made a decision, and the next you're talking yourself out of it."

I fiddle with a crease in my hospital gown and grimace. "When you asked if I'd ever just 'lived', I'd have to say no. If I still have a job in LA, the sensible side of me says I should go back so I can provide for myself."

"I can support you, Maeve."

Pursing my lips, I shake my head. "I've had only myself to rely on for so long, I don't have it in me to depend on anyone else."

He leans forward, clasping his hands between his legs. When he looks up, there's a quirk to the side of his mouth. "What if there was a way you could stay here, explore wherever this is going with us, but still have a salary coming in so you could support yourself?"

I match his half-smile. "We might have spent time in a dream world, but this is real life." Looking at him wryly, I add, "I think." As he chuckles, I shrug. "Maybe I could find a new job if I looked for one, but I can't bank on that."

"What if there was a job already available to you?" His brow rises. I just stare at him, perplexed. "Look, I know you're hesitant about the MC, but the Satan's Devils run their businesses aboveboard. We may not abide by all government rules, but we pay taxes, and someone has to deal with that. We have a construction company, as you know, a tattoo parlour, a strip club, an auto shop and," he gives a small laugh, "Tash, Blade's woman, is an author. Bullet's woman has her own hairdressing business, and every one of those needs someone to do their accounts." He's caught my attention. I didn't know they had so many interests.

"I've been talking to Wizard, our prez."

My eyes crease. "I thought Drummer was your prez?"

"Wiz was wiped out in the same accident that I was. He's still in this hospital, on the next floor, with a badly bruised spine and two broken legs. But he's healing, and soon he'll be back at the helm. Not that Drummer wouldn't probably agree, but it's Wizard who'll have the final say." He glances at me to see if I'm listening. I am. I'm hanging on his every word. "Dollar, our treasurer, wants to step down from his role, but hasn't been allowed to as there was no one to take his place." Quickly, he clarifies, "He'd still have his seat at the table, still report to the club. But you'd be the club's accountant doing all the hard work behind the scenes." He finishes, and his head tilts.

I'd be their accountant? Though I wouldn't be reporting to the club itself, that would still be this Dollar's job. Not so much different in any accountancy firm, where it's the directors who call the shots and report to the board, while people like me get on with the daily slog.

He can see I'm considering it. "There'd be a decent salary attached."

"Like what?" I ask, interested. I'm a money person of course.

Grinning, as if to see I've taken, or am at least circling the bait, he clarifies, "To be negotiated, but I'm sure it wouldn't disappoint."

Part of me wants to jump right in and take it. The sensible portion of my brain tells me to wait. And the side of me that Hound brings out, asks innocently, "And would you be part of the incentive?"

Rising, he doesn't bother with his crutches and hops his

way to the bed. Leaning over, his mesmerising eyes make contact with mine. "Darlin', I'm the main benefit."

His mouth is so close, I can't help but reach my hand to his head, pulling him down to me, sighing as our mouths meet. As our kiss deepens, and he takes charge, arousal floods through me, making my nipples peak through the thin hospital gown. When his hands, drawn by what his eyes see, tease those peaks through the material, quickly following up by applying his talented mouth, I know I'm about to throw all caution to the wind and accept everything the Satan's Devils have to offer.

Hound makes me feel alive.

Only just able to frame words, I gasp, "And can you describe exactly what your benefits comprise of?"

He raises his head only to leer at me. "My house, my bed, my cock. The bitch seat on my bike. My patch on your back, and possibly even a ring on your finger if that's what you want. Maybe a couple of rug rats if that's in our future."

"It's too soon to promise anything." My words are the right ones, the old cautious me. But the new me wants everything he offers, and more.

I'd given up on the idea of ever having a man of my own, thought I'd never be brave enough to take the plunge. I tell myself I need time to think about his and the club's offer, to work out all the pros and the cons. But honestly, is this gift horse any wilder than the experiences Hound and I have already shared? Perhaps this is one time I shouldn't look too closely in its mouth.

I'm capable of only giving him one answer, and a short one at that. "Yes."

My word unlocks a beast in him. He leans over me, pressing me into the bed, his lips on mine, his hands everywhere, and I'm replicating his actions, urging him on. It's heading for a repeat of our interactions in the house when we're interrupted by a shocked gasp.

"Ms. Sullivan, sir, please remember where you are." The nurse is clearly having conniptions. She has a pinched look to her face. "Sir, please remove yourself from Ms. Sullivan's bed, else I'm going to have to call security to escort you out."

With laughter in his eyes, Hound eases himself away. Hopefully, it's only me who can see him adjusting himself in his jeans. *Tomorrow*, he mouths at me.

I can't wait.

With no equipment still attached to me, the nurse has to complete her assessment the old-fashioned way—a blood pressure cuff, a thermometer, and a hand to my pulse. Luckily, she makes no comment on my increased heart rate, and sensibly, seeing what she'd just interrupted. I mean, with a male specimen like Hound, who wouldn't be affected?

When she finally exits, pointedly leaving the door open, Hound and I look at each other. I giggle, he chuckles, then repeats his promise. "Tomorrow, in my bed."

To remove temptation, I slide myself under the sheet, my foot catching something and sending it to the floor. Hound picks it up. It's my phone. He hands it to me.

Unlocking it with my face, I check my emails once again. Drawing in a sharp breath, I tell him, "Under the circumstances, they're holding my position open for me."

I hear Hound's *fuck* murmured under his breath, and see his eyes fill with disappointment.

I don't lead him on. "Which means I'll have to resign my position, effective immediately."

"Fuck, woman," he snarls, brushing his hands through his hair. "Talk like that is just going to get us back into trouble with the nurse again."

CHAPTER TWENTY-TWO
HOUND

These last two weeks have been the best of my life.

Maeve discharged herself from the hospital, came straight back to my house, and immediately breathed life into it. I hadn't realised how much it had been missing a woman's touch. At first, she'd only salvaged a few items from a small suitcase in her totalled car, which we'd managed to track down, but then we'd sent the prospects to LA to pack up everything from her apartment. We'd decided not to go ourselves, or rather, I managed to persuade her to obey her doctor's instructions not to overdo things and rest. The medical staff thought there might be a lasting problem with her heart. Maeve and I dismissed that, believing her health problems had ended with the demise of her aunt and that house. As long as the spirits leave us alone, she'll be fine.

Now my house has been transformed, with knick-knacks, cushions, throws and books combining to make this a real home. My kitchen? Well, I thought I knew all the important things about the woman I'd brought into my life, but I had missed something important. She loved to cook and delighted in the kitchen I'd had installed, almost as much as I've enjoyed eating the results.

To top it all off, yesterday I got rid of my cast. I was dismayed at how much muscle wastage there was, and how, when I walked, I still automatically favoured my left leg. But Peg told me he's already developed a routine that will have me fit in no time. Somehow, I suspect that will be worse than the Hell Week I experienced in the Marines.

Last night I was able to make love properly with my woman for the first time, with no impediment between us, and I'd say, she blew my mind. Compatible? Fuck, she's my match in every way. There's not a surface of this house we haven't christened, even though, up to now, we've had to be inventive. I think eating her out on the kitchen table has to be my favourite, or bending her over the couch, or in the shower, when we discovered the stool was strong enough to bear both our weight. Oh, let's face it, I love having her anytime, any way, and she's never had any complaints. Many times, she's the initiator.

And here she is now, looking like a vision in a dress that reveals the curves that are slowly rounding out on her body, as she puts back on the pounds she lost while she was in that coma. My mouth salivates, and my cock stands to attention to the stimuli as rapidly as Pavlov's dog.

"Down, boy." She chuckles as she comes over, goes on tiptoe, plants the palms of her hands on my cheeks, and pulls me down for a kiss. "We've no time if we don't want to be late."

"They wouldn't miss us," I counter.

"Sure," she retorts. "But we need to be down there before the guest of honour. I'll let you see what's under this dress later."

Now she's got me intrigued. I lift her onto the kitchen

counter, smoothing my hands up her thighs. "Fuck me, you're going to kill me, woman." She's wearing stockings and a garter belt.

I stumble and laugh as she pushes me away. "Later," she promises, with a glint in her eyes.

Knowing she won't be dissuaded, and that she's right, I slide on my cut, then pick up hers and hand it to her. I'd wasted no time claiming her, she'd immediately slotted into my life. And, it seems she loves wearing her "Property of Hound" patch, which declares she's mine. A sense of belonging she's not had for some time. On my part? The still-healing tattoo over my heart shows she owns me, too.

It's been a whirlwind, fast, but also so right.

Nothing was normal about how we got together. Though we fudge the story when asked how we met, simply saying it was in the hospital, which at least has a grain of truth. By unspoken agreement, all who were at the Sullivan House on that Halloween night don't speak about it. It's easy to understand why. We'd only be going around in circles trying to come up with an explanation that makes sense. In truth, there isn't one, so there's no need to go searching.

Bullet, Zane and Shooter might wonder how the house had demolished itself, but they had no other option than to agree it was in a worse state than anyone had expected. Neither Drummer, Peg, Blade, Wraith, or I offered any alternative, nor admitted we were there when it came down. Of course, Maeve now owns the plot, or will once Alex has sorted out the legalities, and proven the new will is legit.

The jewels? Well I've installed a safe to hold them. Maeve wants to keep them rather than sell, and I'm in full agreement with her.

Her fist lightly hits my arm. "Stop daydreaming and let's get down to the clubhouse."

In answer, I offer a sharp salute.

Trying hard not to limp, I walk beside her down to the clubhouse. Stepping inside, I spot the huge banner taped up behind the bar sporting the words, *Welcome home.* A few bottles of champagne stand ready to be opened, and it feels right to celebrate this momentous day, although the sparkling stuff is more likely to be devoured by the old ladies than us men. We'll stick to beer and the hard stuff.

The room is packed to the rafters. Maeve gives me a kiss then goes to join the tables which have been pushed together to house the original old ladies, Carmen, Sandy, Sam, Sophie, Darcy, Becca, Charlotte, Tash, Allie and Mariana, the latter who's dragged herself away from Mouse's and her horses for the day. She's accompanied by their daughters, Yiska, Tanya and Maria. Fitting in with them well are the newer additions to the old lady ranks, Gwen and Virginia. Then there's Isabel, Maya, Zoey, Rose, Hope, Lisa, Eliza, Hilda and Alexis. So many club "children," I'm hard-pressed to keep their parents straight. They're mostly grown now, though. Their brothers are also scattered around, or those who could get away to return to Tucson at short notice, Jacob, Mason and Aiden.

Olivia's watching over not only her baby daughter, but also trying to keep Wizard and Amy's kid, Calvin, amused, while Tommy's beaming as he watches them, looking like a proud grandpa. Though when Calvin shows him a toy car, he looks delighted, just like the overgrown kid that he is.

As Maeve heads toward them, I pause for a moment to watch her, happy how quickly she's been welcomed into the pack, and how well she fits in. Not that she had much of a chance with Sam and Sophie all but adopting her. After a lifetime spent mainly alone, Maeve's blossomed as her tribe has expanded around her. Ah, now Alex has found her. Good, I was hoping the two of them would catch up.

"Big day." Joker slaps my back. As usual, Lady is right beside him.

"Certainly is," I respond, and after exchanging chin lifts, move further into the fray. Bullet and Rock are deep in conversation with Dart, who'd moved to San Diego before I joined the club. The trio offers me a three-fingered salute as I pass.

Marvel's blocking my way, and idly rests his hand on my cut for a moment, as I sidle around him.

"Drink, Hound?" Jekyll asks, noticing my approach and having the bartender's attention.

"Beer," I request gratefully. As he passes an opened bottle to me, I raise it to my lips.

"How you doing?" Truck asks, who's standing with Drifter. "Ready for this?"

I'm about to answer when Dollar steps in close and gets my attention. "Glad you patched Maeve so she can't run away. She's taken a load of weight off my shoulders."

"Guess you're an F.O.G. for real now, Brother. You got your pipe and slippers sorted out?"

"Fuck off," he growls, but his grin gives his real feelings away.

Turning, I spy Hawk and Throttle and approach them. Neither is wearing their slings, and both are looking the picture of health. We spend a moment discussing our various recovery journeys and the exercise regime that Peg's going to have us all on.

Mouse waves and winks at me when I catch sight of him.

It's shoulder to shoulder in here now, but no one's complaining. The room is buzzing with laughter and voices, and adding to the cacophony, a jukebox plays rock in the background. If I'm not mistaken, the playlist is one of Peg's.

I've downed half my bottle when a sudden loud whistle pierces the air. All conversation stops, and the music is turned off. As one, we all turn to face the entrance where, framed by Drummer, Wraith, Peg and Blade, Wizard is entering, pushed by Amy in a wheelchair.

Then the hollers, the cries of welcome back, deafen my ears, making me glad all remnants of the headache I'd had for weeks have finally gone away. Wizard's brought into the centre of the room, and ceremoniously, Drummer hands him his cut, the one that proudly bears the *president* patch. Cheers abound.

Again, Drummer whistles, then calls for silence. When someone passes him a beer, he raises it as if in salute.

"The last couple of months have been tricky," he starts. "But we've made our way through. I'd like to officially welcome our rightful president back to the club." He pauses and searches the room. "Get over here, Hound, and you Hawk. Where's Throttle?" Spying him, he beckons, "Get your asses over here."

We elbow our way through the crowd, then form a semi-circle around Wiz.

Drummer steps back, and it's Wizard who starts to talk, his voice firmer and stronger than I expected after all the time he's spent in a hospital bed.

"Brothers, I'm back, and ready to take up the mantle. I might not be ready to ride, but I can sit at the head of the table and put all you fuckers in your place." A round of laughter greets his words. "I'm happy to announce that Hound, Throttle and Hawk will be back by my side." As another round of cheering bursts out, I glow with pride knowing that, while I doubted it for a while, I've now resumed my position as sergeant-at-arms.

Wizard hasn't finished, and he again waves for silence. "I'd like to thank Drummer, Wraith, Peg and Blade who stood up when we were taken down. They've kept this club running, and I was able to heal, knowing it was in safe hands." Being so close to him, I can see his mouth quirk. "So please join me in raising your glasses to the F.O.G.s."

"Hey, that was a secret. They didn't know we called them that!"

"Worst secret in the world, Sam," someone calls back.

Wizard's chuckling, then, while he can still make himself heard, yells out, "Ride Satan's Devils!"

"Satan's Devils ride together," the whole room yells back.

As if that's a signal, the prospects start popping champagne corks, and I take my cue to step back, as everyone wants to greet, talk to, and welcome their president home.

Finding her way over to me, Maeve links her hand through mine. "Love your club," she tells me. "And I love you so much."

Contentment rolls over me, knowing I have everything I could ever want—an old lady who's the other half of me, and the sergeant-at-arms patch on my cut.

How did we get here? Well, maybe I'll take my cue from my brothers and not think too much on that. Though it might, one day, make a good fairy tale to tell our grandkids. But perhaps not too late at night.

ACKNOWLEDGMENTS AND AUTHOR'S NOTE

I've had such fun bringing the F.O.G.s back into the limelight, I hope you enjoyed riding with them again (or meeting them for the first time).

Thanks must go to my beta readers, Jo, Kathy and Sheri who helped me pull the early draft together – I really appreciate you guys. I wasn't sure this book was going to work until you gave me your positive comments.

To my editor, Mary Kern, what can I say that I haven't already? Love working with you, and so much appreciate your support and encouragement.

Darlene Tallman, thank you once again for doing a quick turnaround proofread. I appreciated your help so much.

Once again, I've used the talent of photographer Golden Czermak for the great shot of model Hunter Harden. And of course, grateful thanks got to CT Cover Creations for the amazing cover.

Finally, last as always, but definitely not least, thanks to all of you, my wonderful readers who've taken a chance on this book. If it wasn't for your encouragement, I wouldn't keep writing. I have recently received messages and emails telling me how much you like my books, and I love reading every one. A positive message inspires me to write more.

This book, like all of my works, has been to beta readers, through editing twice, to a proofreader and then to ARC readers, but there could still be the odd typo that's crept through.

Please message me if you've found anything so I have a chance to correct the book. I love to hear from readers, even if you're pointing out something I've got wrong.

If you've enjoyed this book please consider writing a review. Reviews are essential to us authors, and I appreciate and read them all.

Reader group:. https://www.facebook.com/groups/1852824718066605

Newsletter: http://eepurl.com/b1PXO5

Love and peace

Manda

31 Days of Trick or Treat
TEAM BIKERS

Ember Davis – Devil's Haunting
K.L. Ramsey – Monster's Madhouse
Barbara Nolan – Joker's Ghost
Nat Logan – Twist's Raven
Morgan Jane Mitchell – Biker Boo
Marteeka Karland – Bloody Jack's Treat
Kristine Dugger – Black Widow
Deanna L. Rowley – Lucifer
Summer Winters – Trick's Treat
Chelle C. Craze – Echoes of Nevermore
Manda Mellett – Spooked
Naomi Porter – Zombie's Howl-O-Ween
Claire Shaw – A Witchy Spell Ride
Darlene Tallman – Raiding Halloween
Brooke Summers – Haunted by the Storm
Nikki Landis – Reaper's Ride
J. Lynn Lombard – Vows and Violence
Elise Gedicke – Witch Upon a Star
Erin Osborne – Outlawed Treat
Amy Davies – War's Witch
Calia Wilde – Roses are Dead
Jasmine Grant – Runt's Haunted Ride
Sydney Aaliyah Michelle – Point of Infinity
Penny Anglene – Crane's Hallowed Wrath
Quinn Ryder – Haunting Phantom
Jules Ford – The Devil's Hour
Tich Brewster – Fang
Cala Riley – The Devil's Den
Winter Travers – Claimed by Werewolf

TEAM MOBSTERS

Kathleen Kelly – Graveyard Promises
Elle Boon – Hunting Savage
Heather Dahlgren – Halloween Hit
JL Quincy – The Devil's Masked Corruption
Nola Marie – L'amore del Diavolo
D Williams – Trick or Threat
Harley Wylde – Devil's Embrace
Andi Lynn – Haunting the Shadow Man
ER Whyte – Haunt Me With Vengeance
Ruby Carter – Vows and Vendettas
T.O. Smith – Slay Tricksters and Silent Skeletons
Avelyn Paige – The Reaper's Vow
Cleo Browne – Dima's Vision
Dove Cavanaugh King – Samhain Savior
Eve R. Hart – Cursed Encounter
Glenna Maynard – Wicked Vows
H.J. Marshall – The Madman's Nightmare
Sammie Lyra – His Wicked Spell
Kristine Allen – Broomsticks and Bloodstains
Annelise Reynolds – Traitor or Treat
Rae B. Lake – Haunted Nights & Savage Sins
Lynne Leslie – Blood, Bones, and The Bratva Bogeyman
Layne Daniels – Bratva Beast's Boo
E.C. Land – Bloodmoon Hit

OTHER BOOKS BY MANDA MELLETT

Kings of Anarchy MC

Property of Saint

Property of Short (coming Jan 28 2026)

Satan's Devils MC in reading order

Turning Wheels

Drummer's Beat

Slick Running

Targeting Dart

Heart Broken

Peg's Stand

Rock Bottom

Joker's Fool

Mouse Trapped

Paladin's Hell

Blade's Edge

Demon's Angel

Devil's Due

Heart Mended (novella)

Truck Stopped

Devil's Dilemma

Ink's Devil

Devil's Spawn

Being Lost

Road Tripped

Grumbler's Ride

Stormy's Thunder

Avenging Devil Part 1

Avenging Devil Part 2

Red's Peril Part 1

Red's Peril Part 2

Petty's Crime

Second Generation

Amy's Santa

Hawk's Cry

Twisted Throtle

Saving Marvel

Spooked! (Coming October 11 2025) Written as part of the 31 days of Trick or Treat Biker series)

Wicked Warriors MC

Warts an' All

Tickety Tock

Wretched Soulz MC

StoryTeller's Tale

Fire meets Fire

Strider's Misstep

Blood Brothers (Billionaires and their bodyguards)

Stolen Lives

Close Protection

Second Chances

Identity Crisis

Dark Horses

Hard Choices

ABOUT THE AUTHOR

By using the rich fabric of her personal life, psychology degree, varied work experiences, and amazing characters she's met, Manda is able to populate her books with believable in-depth characters and enjoys pitting them against situations which challenge them. Her books are full of suspense, twists and turns and the unexpected.

Manda lives in the beautiful countryside of Somerset in the UK. As well as writing books and reading, Manda loves walking her dog and keeping fit. She lives with her husband of over 30 years, who, along with her son, is her greatest fan and supporter.

Photo by Carmel Jane Photography